1969

e

The Psychiatrist

AND OTHER STORIES

MACHADO DE ASSIS

The Psychiatrist

AND OTHER STORIES

Translated by William L. Grossman & Helen Caldwell

University of California Press / Berkeley & Los Angeles, 1966

University of California Press
Berkeley and Los Angeles
California

Peter Owen Limited
London, England

Second Printing, 1966

Published with the assistance of a grant from the
    Rockefeller Foundation

Library of Congress Catalog Card Number 63–9407

Designed by Theo Jung

Printed in the United States of America

Contents

Introduction

Machado de Assis (1839–1908), the shy, epileptic mulatto who achieved universality within the provincial confines of nineteenth-century Rio de Janeiro, remained virtually unknown in the United States until 1952, when at long last an English translation of one of his novels was published. Now he is recognized here as (in Dudley Fitts's words) "a literary force transcending nationality and language, comparable certainly to Flaubert, Hardy, or James." Two universities in this country now give courses exclusively on his works. An increasing number of readers are coming to share Helen Caldwell's opinion that his *Dom Casmurro* is "perhaps the finest of all American novels of either continent." His *Epitaph of a Small Winner* has been included in great-books courses and enshrined in a library list of One Hundred Great Novels.

According to an eminent Machadian (the late Lúcia Miguel Pereira), however, "it was undoubtedly as a short-story writer that Machado de Assis wrought his masterpieces." Another scholar, Renard Perez, points out that the short story was the ideal form for so meticulous and concise a writer, who liked to attack his themes "vertically." "It is the acuteness of his analyses," says Perez, "together with the originality of his themes and his perfection of form, that make him a world master of the short story."

Yet, although a book of Machado's stories appeared in French as early as 1910, they have been slow to find their way into English. Before the preparation of the present volume, English translations of only five were published. (Three are in Isaac Goldberg's *Brazilian Tales*, long out of print. The other two, my translations of "Midnight Mass" and "Admiral's Night," appeared in *Noonday* and *Harper's Bazaar*, respectively, and are included by permission in this volume.)

In Brazil, probably the most celebrated of the stories here presented is "Midnight Mass." Readers are captivated by its typically Machadian combination of insight, simplicity, and subtlety. It brings to mind a passage in an essay on Machado by the dean of Brazilian intellectuals, Alceu Amoroso Lima: "He writes more between the lines than on the lines. He suggests more than he says. He evokes more than he manifests. And he never writes without an ulterior meaning."

In one of the forty-odd books on Machado de Assis written by Brazilians, Agrippino Grieco remarks the dream-like quality of "Midnight Mass." In another, Gondin da Fonseca notes its "suffocating atmosphere of excitement and frustration," but to him any dreaminess would doubtless be a consequence of the "onanistic sublimation" that he finds in both this story and "A Woman's Arms." He maintains that young Nogueira, the narrator, "although deftly provoked by Conceição, pretends not to recognize her desires and does not possess her, no matter how much she offers herself." But can we be so sure that the narrator was merely pretending? He himself tells us otherwise. And can one be wholly precise about Conceição's objective? Is it so certain that she would have permitted herself to be possessed? The charm of the story derives in part from its mixture of clarity and elusiveness in the interplay of inexplicit desires and restraints. One who tries to make them wholly explicit may tell more about himself than about the story—a danger often encountered in efforts to interpret Machado's stories and novels, especially those told in the first person.

"Education of a Stuffed Shirt" is one of the several works in which Machado ridicules the dedication of men to the superficial, the inauthentic, the mediocre. The formula for success prescribed here by the father—essentially, conformity plus publicity—is chillingly up-to-date. In this vein, Machado has much in common with certain Christian polemicists, although he had no apparent religious motive and there is even considerable doubt about his religious beliefs. For example, the father's guidance to his son is, in some areas, remarkably like the guidance recommended many years later by C. S. Lewis's master devil in *The Screwtape Letters*. The father warns his son not to think out any ideas of his own and counsels him to rely on clichés; Screwtape wants a man to be directed away from the use of reason and to be made dependent upon the current jargon that replaces individual thought. Even in concrete detail there are parallels: both the father and Screwtape warn against unaccompanied walks and against the reading of authoritative works on science.

In temperament and basic emphasis, however, Machado was closer to Kierkegaard—whom he doubtless never read. With much the same intensity and sometimes with similar thrusts of caustic wit, these two strange prophets remind us that we must be judged as individuals, not as parts of the crowd, that merger into the mass cannot free us of our responsibility to choose the true and the authentic. The bonds between Machado and still other religious writers are not hard to recognize and some have been pointed out: a Brazilian scholar (Afrânio Coutinho) has examined the influence of Pascal on Machado, and an American nun (Sister M. John Berchmans Kocher), in a doctoral dissertation, has studied the relationship between Machado and the author of *Ecclesiastes.*

In a brilliant series of studies on the influence of English writers on Machado, Eugênio Gomes indicates that the theme of "The Psychiatrist" may well have been suggested by Swift's *A Serious and Useful Scheme to Make an Hospital for Incurables.* "But," says Gomes, "the satire in 'The Psychiatrist' goes much farther than Swift's: it virtually obliterates the boundary between reason and madness."

Like others of Machado's works, this story means somewhat different things to different exegetes. According to Augusto Meyer, its satire is aimed at "mental activity itself" and especially at pure rationalism, represented in the story by Dr. Bacamarte. Barreto Filho finds in "The Psychiatrist" not only Machado's contempt for "scientific rationalism" and for "scientific dictatorship" but also an attack upon specifically Brazilian ways of thinking. "Anyone," he writes, "who knows our receptivity to everything that presents itself in the guise of science, our readiness to plunge into improbable projects, anyone who observes how little resistance we have to imported theories of politics or pedagogy—in brief, our delight in panaceas—knows what Machado de Assis was seeking to stigmatize. . . ."

Without denying the validity of these interpretations, so far as they go, I wonder whether the central thought of the story is not in an observation by Pascal: "Men are so necessarily mad, that not to be mad would amount to another form of madness." By a curious coincidence, four-fifths of the people in Itaguai were found by Dr. Bacamarte to be mentally ill, and four-fifths of the persons residing in a certain part of Manhattan were recently found by investigators to be not "free enough of emotional symptoms to be considered well."

Taken together, these and the nine other stories provide a fair, although of course not wholly representative, sample of Machado's concepts and methods. We see his economy of means and his sometimes deceptive simplicity. We see his hatred of cruelty, his sympathetic understanding of young people (rarely reciprocated), his perception of hidden and even unconscious motives, his lack of interest in inanimate nature ("Where are the trees?" complained one reader), his curiosity about the relationship between good and evil—and always his critique, now biting, now compassionate, of human inadequacy.

WILLIAM L. GROSSMAN

The Psychiatrist

I. How Itaguai Acquired a Madhouse

The chronicles of Itaguai relate that in remote times a certain physician of noble birth, Simão Bacamarte, lived there and that he was one of the greatest doctors in all Brazil, Portugal, and the Spains. He had studied for many years in both Padua and Coimbra. When, at the age of thirty-four, he announced his decision to return to Brazil and his home town of Itaguai, the King of Portugal tried to dissuade him; he offered Bacamarte his choice between the Presidency of Coimbra University and the office of Chief Expediter of Government Affairs. The doctor politely declined.

"Science," he told His Majesty, "is my only office; Itaguai, my universe."

He took up residence there and dedicated himself to the theory and practice of medicine. He alternated therapy with study and research; he demonstrated theorems with poultices.

In his fortieth year Bacamarte married the widow of a circuit judge. Her name was Dona Evarista da Costa e Mascarenhas, and she was neither beautiful nor charming. One of his uncles, an outspoken man, asked him why he had not selected a more attractive woman. The doctor replied that Dona Evarista enjoyed perfect digestion, excellent eyesight, and normal blood pressure; she had had no serious illnesses and her urinalysis was negative. It was likely she would give him healthy, robust children. If, in addition to her physiological accomplishments, Dona Evarista possessed a face composed of features neither individually pretty nor mutually compatible, he thanked God for it, for he would not be tempted to sacrifice his scientific pursuits to the contemplation of his wife's attractions.

But Dona Evarista failed to satisfy her husband's expectations. She produced no robust children and, for that matter, no puny ones either. The scientific temperament is by nature patient; Bacamarte waited three, four, five years. At the end of this period he began an exhaustive study of sterility. He reread the works of all the authorities (including the Arabian), sent inquiries to the Italian and German universities, and finally recommended a special diet. But Dona Evarista, nourished almost exclusively on succulent Itaguai pork, paid no heed; and to this lack of wifely submissiveness—understandable but regrettable—we owe the total extinction of the Bacamartian dynasty.

The pursuit of science is sometimes itself therapeutic. Dr. Bacamarte cured himself of his disappointment by plunging even deeper into his work. It was at this time that one of the byways of medicine attracted his attention: psychopathology. The entire colony and, for that matter, the kingdom itself could not boast one authority on the subject. It was a field, indeed, in which little responsible work had been done anywhere in the world. Simão Bacamarte saw an opportunity for Lusitanian and, more specifically, Brazilian science to cover itself with "imperishable laurels"—an expression he himself used, but only in a moment of ecstasy and within the confines of his home; to the outside world he was always modest and restrained, as befits a man of learning.

"The health of the soul!" he exclaimed. "The loftiest possible goal for a doctor."

"For a great doctor like yourself, yes." This emendation came from Crispim Soares, the town druggist and one of Bacamarte's most intimate friends.

The chroniclers chide the Itaguai Town Council for its neglect of the mentally ill. Violent madmen were locked up at home; peaceable lunatics were simply left at large; and none, violent or peaceable, received care of any sort. Simão Bacamarte proposed to change all this. He decided to build an asylum and he asked the Council for authority to receive and treat all the mentally ill of Itaguai and the surrounding area. He would be paid by the patient's family or, if the family was very poor, by the Council. The proposal aroused excitement and curiosity throughout the town. There was considerable opposition, for it is always difficult to uproot the established way of doing things, however absurd or evil it may be. The idea of having madmen live together in the same house seemed itself to be a symptom of madness, as many intimated even to the doctor's wife.

"Look, Dona Evarista," said Father Lopes, the local vicar, "see if you can't get your husband to take a little holiday. In Rio de Janeiro, maybe. All this intensive study, a man can take just so much of it and then his mind . . ."

Dona Evarista was terrified. She went to her husband and said that she had a consuming desire to take a trip with him to Rio de Janeiro. There, she said, she would eat whatever he thought necessary for the attainment of a certain objective. But the astute doctor immediately perceived what was on his wife's mind and replied that she need have no fear. He then went to the town hall, where the Council was debating his proposal, which he supported with such eloquence that it was approved without amendment on the first ballot. The Council also adopted a tax designed to pay for the lodging, sustenance, and treatment of the indigent mad. This involved a bit of a problem, for everything in Itaguai was already being taxed. After considerable study the Council authorized the use of two plumes on the horses drawing a funeral coach. Anyone wishing to take advantage of this privilege would pay a tax of a stated amount for each hour from the time of death to the termination of the rites at the grave. The town clerk was asked to determine the probable revenue from the new tax, but he got lost in arithmetical calculations, and one of the Councilmen, who was opposed to the doctor's undertaking, suggested that the clerk be relieved of a useless task.

"The calculations are unnecessary," he said, "because Dr. Bacamarte's project will never be executed. Who ever heard of putting a lot of crazy people together in one house?"

But the worthy Councilman was wrong. Bacamarte built his madhouse on New Street, the finest thoroughfare in Itaguai. The building had a courtyard in the center and two hundred cubicles, each with one window. The doctor, an ardent student of Arabian lore, found a passage in the Koran in which Mohammed declared that the insane were holy, for Allah had deprived them of their judgment in order to keep them from sinning. Bacamarte found the idea at once beautiful and profound, and he had the passage engraved on the façade of the house. But he feared that this might offend the Vicar and, through him, the Bishop. Accordingly, he attributed the quotation to Benedict VIII.

The asylum was called the Green House, for its windows were the first of that color ever seen in Itaguai. The formal opening was celebrated magnificently. People came from the entire region, some even from Rio de Janeiro, to witness the ceremonies, which lasted seven days. Some patients had already been admitted, and their relatives took advantage of this opportunity to observe the paternal care and Christian charity with which they were treated. Dona Evarista, delighted by her husband's glory, covered herself with silks, jewels, and flowers. She was a real queen during those memorable days. Everyone came to visit her two or three times. People not only paid court to her but praised her, for—and this fact does great honor to the society of the time—they thought of Dona Evarista in terms of the lofty spirit and prestige of her husband; they envied her, to be sure, but with the noble and blessed envy of admiration.

II. A Torrent of Madmen

Three days later, talking in an expansive mood with the druggist Crispim Soares, the psychiatrist revealed his inmost thoughts.

"Charity, Soares, definitely enters into my method. It is the seasoning in the recipe, for thus I interpret the words of St. Paul to the Corinthians: 'Though I understand all mysteries and all knowledge . . . and have not charity, I am nothing.' But the main thing in my work at the Green House is to study insanity in depth, to learn its various gradations, to classify the various cases, and finally to discover the cause of the phenomenon and its remedy. This is my heart's desire. I believe that in this way I can render a valuable service to humanity."

"A great service," said Crispim Soares.

"Without this asylum," continued the psychiatrist, "I might conceivably accomplish a little. But it provides far greater scope and opportunity for my studies than I would otherwise have."

"Far greater," agreed the druggist.

And he was right. From all the towns and villages in the vicinity came the violent, the depressed, the monomaniacal—the mentally ill of every type and variety. At the end of four months the Green House was a little community in itself. A gallery with thirty-seven more cubicles had to be added. Father Lopes confessed that he had not imagined there were so many madmen in the world nor that such strange cases of madness existed. One of the patients, a coarse, ignorant young man, gave a speech every day after lunch. It was an academic discourse, with metaphors, antitheses, and apostrophes, ornamented with Greek words and quotations from Cicero, Apuleius, and Tertullian. The Vicar could hardly believe his ears. What, a fellow he had seen only three months ago hanging around street corners!

"Quite so," replied the psychiatrist. "But Your Reverence has observed for himself. This happens every day."

"The only explanation I can think of," said the priest, "is the confusion of languages on the Tower of Babel. They were so completely mixed together that now, probably, when a man loses his reason, he easily slips from one into another."

"That may well be the divine explanation," agreed the psychiatrist after a moment's reflection, "but I'm looking for a purely scientific, human explanation—and I believe there is one."

"Maybe so, but I really can't imagine what it could be."

Several of the patients had been driven mad by love. One of these spent all his time wandering through the building and courtyard in search of his wife, whom he had killed in a fit of jealousy that marked the beginning of his insanity. Another thought he was the morning star. He had repeatedly proposed marriage to a certain young lady, and she had continually put him off. He knew why: she thought him dreadfully dull and was waiting to see if she could catch a more interesting husband. So he became a brilliant star, standing with feet and arms outspread like rays. He would remain in this position for hours, waiting to be supplanted by the rising sun.

There were some noteworthy cases of megalomania. One patient, the son of a cheap tailor, invented a genealogy in which he traced his ancestry back to members of royalty and, through them, ultimately to Jehovah. He would recite the entire list of his male progenitors, with a "begat" to link each father and son. Then he would slap his forehead, snap his fingers, and say it all over again. Another patient had a somewhat similar idea but developed it with more rigorous logic. Beginning with the proposition that he was a child of God, which even the Vicar would not have denied, he reasoned that, as the species of the child is the same as that of the parent, he himself must be a god. This conclusion, derived from two irrefutable premises—one Biblical, the other scientific—placed him far above the lunatics who identified themselves with Caesar, Alexander, or other mere mortals.

More remarkable even than the manias and delusions of the madmen was the patience of the psychiatrist. He began by engaging two administrative assistants—an idea that he accepted from Crispim Soares along with the druggist's two nephews. He gave these young men the task of enforcing the rules and regulations that the Town Council had approved for the asylum. They also kept the records and were in charge of the distribution of food and clothing. Thus, the doctor was free to devote all his time to psychiatry.

"The Green House," he told the Vicar, "now has its temporal government and its spiritual government." *

Father Lopes laughed. "What a delightful novelty," he said, "to find a society in which the spiritual dominates."

Relieved of administrative burdens, Dr. Bacamarte began an exhaustive study of each patient: his personal and family history, his habits, his likes and dislikes, his hobbies, his attitudes toward others, and so on. He also spent long hours studying, inventing, and experimenting with psychotherapeutic methods. He slept little and ate little; and while he ate he was still working, for at the dinner table he would read an old text or ponder a difficult problem. Often he sat through an entire dinner without saying a word to Dona Evarista.

III. God Knows What He Is Doing

By the end of two months the psychiatrist's wife was the most wretched of women. She did not reproach her husband but suffered in silence. She declined into a state of deep melancholy, became thin and yellowish, ate little, and sighed continually. One day, at dinner, he asked what was wrong with her. She sadly replied that it was nothing. Then she ventured for the first time

* A play on words, for *espiritual* means both "spiritual" and "pertaining to the mind."

to complain a little, saying she considered herself as much a widow now as before she married him.

"Who would ever have thought that a bunch of lunatics . . ."

She did not complete the sentence. Or, rather, she completed it by raising her eyes to the ceiling. Dona Evarista's eyes were her most attractive feature—large, black, and bathed in a vaporous light like the dawn. She had used them in much the same way when trying to get Simão Bacamarte to propose. Now she was brandishing her weapon again, this time for the apparent purpose of cutting science's throat. But the psychiatrist was not perturbed. His eyes remained steady, calm, enduring. No wrinkle disturbed his brow, as serene as the waters of Botafogo Bay. Perhaps a slight smile played on his lips as he said:

"You may go to Rio de Janeiro."

Dona Evarista felt as if the floor had vanished and she were floating on air. She had never been to Rio, which, although hardly a shadow of what it is today, was, by comparison with Itaguai, a great and fascinating metropolis. Ever since childhood she had dreamed of going there. She longed for Rio as a Hebrew in the captivity must have longed for Jerusalem, but with her husband settled so definitively in Itaguai she had lost hope. And now, of a sudden, he was permitting her to realize her dream. Dona Evarista could not hide her elation. Simão Bacamarte took her by the hand and smiled in a manner at once conjugal and philosophical.

"How strange is the therapy of the soul!" he thought. "This lady is wasting away because she thinks I do not love her. I give her Rio de Janeiro and she is well again." And he made a note of the phenomenon.

A sudden misgiving pierced Dona Evarista's heart. She concealed her anxiety, however, and merely told her husband that, if he did not go, neither would she, for of course she could not travel alone.

"Your aunt will go with you," replied the psychiatrist.

It should be noted that this expedient had occurred to Dona Evarista. She had not suggested it, for it would impose great expense on her husband. Besides, it was better for the suggestion to come from him.

"Oh, but the money it will cost!" she sighed.

"It doesn't matter," he replied. "Have you any idea of our income?"

He brought her the books of account. Dona Evarista, although impressed by the quantity of the figures, was not quite sure what they signified, so her husband took her to the chest where the money was kept.

Good heavens! There were mountains of gold, thousands upon thousands of cruzados and doubloons. A fortune! While she was drinking it in with her black eyes, the psychiatrist placed his mouth close to her and whispered mischievously:

" 'Who would ever have thought that a bunch of lunatics . . .' "

Dona Evarista understood, smiled, and replied with infinite resignation:

"God knows what he is doing."

Three months later she left for Rio in the company of her aunt, the druggist's wife, one of the druggist's cousins, a priest whom Bacamarte had known in Lisbon and who happened to be in Itaguaí, four maidservants, and five or six male attendants. A small crowd had come to see them off. The farewells were sad for everyone but the psychiatrist, for he was troubled by nothing outside the realm of science. Even Dona Evarista's tears, sincere and abundant as they were, did not affect him. If anything concerned him on that occasion, if he cast a restless and police-like eye over the crowd, it was only because he suspected the presence of one or two candidates for commitment to the Green House.

After the departure the druggist and the psychiatrist mounted their horses and rode homeward. Crispim Soares stared at the road, between the ears of his roan. Simão Bacamarte swept the horizon with his eyes, surveyed the distant mountains, and let his horse find the way home. Perfect symbols of the common man and of the genius! One fixes his gaze upon the present with all its tears and privations; the other looks beyond to the glorious dawns of a future that he himself will shape.

IV. A New Theory

As his horse jogged along, a new and daring hypothesis occurred to Simão Bacamarte. It was so daring, indeed, that, if substantiated, it would revolutionize the bases of psychopathology. During the next few days he mulled it over. Then, in his spare time, he began to go from house to house, talking with the townspeople about a thousand and one things and punctuating the conversations with a penetrating look that terrified even the bravest.

One morning, after this had been going on for about three weeks, Crispim Soares received a message that the psychiatrist wished to see him.

"He says it's important," added the messenger.

The druggist turned pale. Something must have happened to his wife! The chroniclers of Itaguai, it should be noted, dwell upon Crispim's love for his Cesaria and point out that they had never been separated in their thirty years of marriage. Only against this background can one explain the monologue, often overheard by the servants, with which the druggist reviled himself: "You miss your wife, do you? You're going crazy without her? It serves you right! Always truckling to Dr. Bacamarte! Who told you to let Cesaria go traveling? Dr. Bacamarte, that's who. Anything he says, you say amen. So now see what you get for it, you vile, miserable, groveling little lackey! Lickspittle! Flunky!" And he added many other ugly names that a man ought not call his enemies, much less himself. The effect of the message on him, in this state of mind, can be readily imagined. He dropped the drugs he had been mixing and fairly flew to the Green House. Simão Bacamarte greeted him joyfully, but he wore his joy as a wise man should—buttoned up to the neck with circumspection.

"I am very happy," he said.

"Some news of our wives?" asked the druggist in a tremulous voice.

The psychiatrist made a magnificent gesture and replied:

"It is something much more important—a scientific experiment. I say 'experiment,' for I do not yet venture to affirm the correctness of my theory. Indeed, this is the very nature of science, Soares: unending inquiry. But, although only an experiment as yet, it may change the face of the earth. Till now, madness has been thought a small island in an ocean of sanity. I am beginning to suspect that it is not an island at all but a continent."

He fell silent for a while, enjoying the druggist's amazement. Then he explained his theory at length. The number of persons suffering from insanity, he believed, was far greater than commonly supposed; and he developed this idea with an abundance of reasons, texts, and examples. He found many of these examples in Itaguai, but he recognized the fallacy of confining his data to one time and place and he therefore resorted to history. He pointed in particular to certain historical celebrities: Socrates, who thought he had a personal demon; Pascal, who sewed a report of an hallucination into the lining of his coat; Mohammed, Caracalla, Domitian, Caligula, and others. The druggist's surprise at Bacamarte's mingling of the vicious and the merely ridiculous moved the psychiatrist to explain that these apparently inconsistent attributes were really different aspects of the same thing.

"The grotesque, my friend, is simply ferocity in disguise."

"Clever, very clever!" exclaimed Crispim Soares.

As for the basic idea of enlarging the realm of insanity, the druggist found it a little far-fetched; but modesty, his chief virtue, kept him from stating his opinion. Instead, he expressed a noble enthusiasm. He declared the idea sublime and added that it was "something for the noisemaker." This expression requires explanation. Like the other towns, villages, and settlements in the colony at that time, Itaguai had no newspaper. It used two media for the publication of news: hand-written posters nailed to the doors of the town hall and of the main church, and the noisemaker.

This is how the latter medium worked: a man was hired for one or more days to go through the streets rattling a noisemaker. A crowd would gather and the man would announce whatever he had been paid to announce: a cure for malaria, a gift to the Church, some farm land for sale, and the like. He might even be engaged to read a sonnet to the people. The system continually disturbed the peace of the community, but it survived a long time because of its almost miraculous effectiveness. Incredible as it may seem, the noisemaker actually enabled merchants to sell inferior goods at superior prices and third-rate authors to pass as geniuses. Yes, indeed, not all the institutions of the old regime deserve our century's contempt.

"No, I won't announce my theory to the public," replied the psychiatrist. "I'll do something better: I'll act on it."

The druggist agreed that it might be best to begin that way. "There'll be plenty of time for the noisemaker afterwards," he concluded.

But Simão Bacamarte was not listening. He seemed lost in meditation. When he finally spoke, it was with great deliberation.

"Think of humanity," he said, "as a great oyster shell. Our first task, Soares, is to extract the pearl—that is, reason. In other words, we must determine the nature and boundaries of reason. Madness is simply all that lies beyond those limits. But what is reason if not the equilibrium of the mental faculties? An individual, therefore, who lacks this equilibrium in any particular is, to that extent, insane."

Father Lopes, to whom he also confided his theory, replied that he was not quite sure he understood it but that it sounded a little dangerous and, in any case, would involve more work than one doctor could possibly handle.

"Under the present definition of insanity, which has always been accepted," he added, "the fence around the area is perfectly clear and satisfactory. Why not stay within it?"

The vague suggestion of a smile played on the fine and discreet lips of the psychiatrist, a smile in which disdain blended with pity. But he said nothing. Science merely extended its hand to theology—with such assurance that theology was undecided whether to believe in itself or in science. Itaguai and the entire world were on the brink of a revolution.

V. The Terror

Four days later the population of Itaguai was dismayed to hear that a certain Mr. Costa had been committed to the Green House.

"Impossible!"

"What do you mean, impossible! They took him away this morning."

Costa was one of the most highly esteemed citizens of Itaguai. He had inherited 400,000 cruzados in the good coin of King João V. As his uncle said in the will, the interest on this capital would have been enough to support him "till the end of the world." But as soon as he received the inheritance he began to make loans to people without interest: a thousand cruzados to one, two thousand to another, three hundred to another, eight hundred to another, until, at the end of five years, there was nothing left. If poverty had come to him all at once, the shock to the good people of Itaguai would have been enormous. But it came gradually. He went from opulence to wealth, from wealth to

comfort, from comfort to indigence, and from indigence to poverty. People who, five years earlier, had always doffed their hats
and bowed deeply to him as soon as they saw him a block away,
now clapped him on the shoulder, flicked him on the nose, and
made coarse remarks. But Costa remained affable, smiling, sub-
limely resigned. He was untroubled even by the fact that the
least courteous were the very ones who owed him money; on the
contrary, he seemed to greet them with especial pleasure.

Once, when one of these eternal debtors jeered at him and
Costa merely smiled, someone said to him: "You're nice to this
fellow because you still hope you can get him to pay what he
owes you." Costa did not hesitate an instant. He went to the
debtor and forgave the debt. "Sure," said the man who had made
the unkind remark, "Costa canceled the debt because he knew he
couldn't collect it anyway." Costa was no fool; he had anticipated
this reaction. Inventive and jealous of his honor, he found a way
two hours later to prove the slur unmerited: he took a few coins
and loaned them to the same debtor.

"Now I hope . . . ," he thought.

This act of Costa's convinced the credulous and incredulous
alike. Thereafter no one doubted the nobility of spirit of that
worthy citizen. All the needy, no matter how timid, came in their
patched cloaks and knocked on his door. The words of the man
who had impugned his motive continued, however, to gnaw like
worms at his soul. But this also ended, for three months later
the man asked him for one hundred and twenty cruzados, promis-
ing to repay it in two days. This was all that remained of the
inheritance, but Costa made the loan immediately, without hesitation or interest. It was a means of noble redress for the stain on
his honor. In time the debt might have been paid; unfortunately,
Costa could not wait, for five months later he was committed to
the Green House.

The consternation in Itaguai, when the matter became known,
can readily be imagined. No one spoke of anything else. Some
said that Costa had gone mad during lunch, others said it had
happened early in the morning. They told of the mental attacks
he had suffered, described by some as violent and frightening, by
others as mild and even amusing. Many people hurried to the
Green House. There they found poor Costa calm if somewhat
surprised, speaking with great lucidity and asking why he had

been brought there. Some went and talked with the psychiatrist. Bacamarte approved of their esteem and compassion for the patient, but he explained that science was science and that he could not permit a madman to remain at large. The last person to intercede (for, after what I am about to relate, no one dared go to see the dreadful psychiatrist) was a lady cousin of the patient. The doctor told her that Costa must certainly be insane, for otherwise he would not have thrown away all the money that . . .

"No! Now there you are wrong!" interrupted the good woman energetically. "He was not to blame for what he did."

"No?"

"No, Doctor. I'll tell you exactly what happened. My uncle was not ordinarily a bad man, but when he became angry he was so fierce that he would not even take off his hat to a religious procession. Well, one day, a short time before he died, he discovered that a slave had stolen an ox from him. His face became as red as a pepper; he shook from head to foot; he foamed at the mouth. Then an ugly, shaggy-haired man came up to him and asked for a drink of water. My uncle (may God show him the light!) told the man to go drink in the river—or in hell, for all he cared. The man glared at him, raised his hand threateningly, and uttered this curse: 'Your money will not last more than seven years and a day, as surely as this is the star of David!' And he showed a star of David tattooed on his arm. That was the cause of it all, Doctor—the hex put on the money by that evil man."

Bacamarte's eyes pierced the poor woman like daggers. When she had finished, he extended his hand as courteously as if she had been the wife of the Viceroy and invited her to go and talk with her cousin. The miserable woman believed him. He took her to the Green House and locked her up in the ward for those suffering from delusions or hallucinations.

When this duplicity on the part of the illustrious Bacamarte became known, the townspeople were terrified. No one could believe that, for no reason at all, the psychiatrist would lock up a perfectly sane woman whose only offense had been to intercede on behalf of an unfortunate relative. The case was gossiped about on street corners and in barber shops. Within a short time it developed into a full-scale novel, with amorous overtures by the psychiatrist to Costa's cousin, Costa's indignation, the cousin's scorn, and finally the psychiatrist's vengeance on them both. It was all very obvious. But did not the doctor's austerity and his life of devotion to science give the lie to such a story? Not at all! This was merely a cloak by which he concealed his treachery. And one of the more credulous of the townspeople even whispered that he knew certain other things—he would not say what, for he lacked complete proof—but he knew they were true, he could almost swear to them.

"You who are his intimate friend," they asked the druggist, "can't you tell us what's going on, what happened, what reason . . . ?"

Crispim Soares was delighted. This questioning by his puzzled friends, and by the uneasy and curious in general, amounted to public recognition of his importance. There was no doubt about it, the entire population knew that he, Crispim the druggist, was the psychiatrist's confidant, the great man's collaborator. That is why they all came running to the pharmacy. All this could be read in the druggist's jocund expression and discreet smile—and in his silence, for he made no reply. One, two, perhaps three dry monosyllables at the most, cloaked in a loyal, constant half-smile and full of scientific mysteries which he could reveal to no human being without danger and dishonor.

"There's something very strange going on," thought the townspeople.

But one of them merely shrugged his shoulders and went on his way. He had more important interests. He had just built a magnificent house, with a garden that was a masterpiece of art and taste. His furniture, imported from Hungary and Holland, was visible from the street, for the windows were always open. This man, who had become rich in the manufacture of packsaddles, had always dreamed of owning a sumptuous house, an elaborate garden, and rare furniture. Now he had acquired all these things and, in semi-retirement, was devoting most of his time to the enjoyment of them. His house was undoubtedly the finest in Itaguai, more grandiose than the Green House, nobler than the town hall. There was wailing and gnashing of teeth among Itaguai's social elite whenever they heard it praised or even mentioned—indeed, when they even thought about it. Owned by a mere manufacturer of packsaddles, good God!

"There he is, staring at his own house," the passers-by would say. For it was his custom to station himself every morning in the middle of his garden and gaze lovingly at the house. He would keep this up for a good hour, until called in to lunch.

Although his neighbors always greeted him respectfully enough, they would laugh behind his back. One of them observed that Mateus could make a lot more money manufacturing pack-saddles to put on himself—a somewhat unintelligible remark, which nevertheless sent the listeners into ecstasies of laughter.

Every afternoon, when the families went out for their after-dinner walks (people dined early in those days), Mateus would station himself at the center window, elegantly clothed in white against a dark background. He would remain there in a majestic pose for three or four hours, until it was dark. One may reasonably infer an intention on Mateus's part to be admired and envied, although he confessed no such purpose to anyone, not even to Father Lopes. His good friend the druggist nevertheless drew the inference and communicated it to Bacamarte. The psychiatrist suggested that, as the saddler's house was of stone, he might have been suffering from petrophilia, an illness that the doctor had discovered and had been studying for some time. This continual gazing at the house . . .

"No, Doctor," interrupted Crispim Soares vigorously.

"No?"

"Pardon me, but perhaps you don't know . . ." And he told the psychiatrist what the saddler did every afternoon.

Simão Bacamarte's eyes lighted up with scientific voluptuousness. He questioned Crispim at some length, and the answers he received were apparently satisfactory, even pleasant, to him. But there was no suggestion of a sinister intent in the psychiatrist's face or manner—quite the. contrary—as he asked the druggist's arm for a little stroll in the afternoon sun. It was the first time he had bestowed this honor on his confidant. Crispim, stunned and trembling, accepted the invitation. Just then, two or three people came to see the doctor. Crispim silently consigned them to all the devils. They were delaying the walk; Bacamarte might even take it into his head to invite one of them in Crispim's stead. What impatience! What anxiety! Finally the visitors left and the two men set out on their walk. The psychiatrist chose the direction of Mateus's house. He strolled by the window five or six times, slowly, stopping now and then and observing the saddler's physical attitude and facial expression. Poor Mateus noticed only that he was an object of the curiosity or admiration of the most important figure in Itaguai. He intensified the nobility of his expression, the stateliness of his pose. . . . Alas! he was merely helping to condemn himself. The next day he was committed.

"The Green House is a private prison," said an unsuccessful doctor.

Never had an opinion caught on and spread so rapidly. "A private prison"—the words were repeated from one end of Itaguai to the other. Fearfully, to be sure, for during the week following the Mateus episode twenty-odd persons, including two or three of the town's prominent citizens, had been committed to the Green House. The psychiatrist said that only the mentally ill were admitted, but few believed him. Then came the popular explanations of the matter: revenge, greed, a punishment from God, a monomania afflicting the doctor himself, a secret plan on the part of Rio de Janeiro to destroy the budding prosperity of Itaguai and ultimately to impoverish this rival municipality, and a thousand other products of the public imagination.

At this time the party of travelers returned from their visit of several weeks to Rio de Janeiro. The psychiatrist, the druggist, Father Lopes, the Councilmen, and several other officials went to greet them. The moment when Dona Evarista laid eyes again on her husband is regarded by the chroniclers of the time as one of the most sublime instants in the moral history of man, because of the contrast between these two extreme (although both commendable) natures. Dona Evarista uttered a cry, stammered a word or two, and threw herself at her husband in a way that suggested at once the fierceness of a wildcat and the gentle affection of a dove. Not so the noble Bacamarte. With diagnostic objectivity, without disturbing for a moment his scientific austerity, he extended his arms to the lady, who fell into them and fainted. The incident was brief; two minutes later Dona Evarista's friends were greeting her and the homeward procession began.

The psychiatrist's wife was Itaguai's great hope. Everyone counted on her to alleviate the scourge. Hence the public acclamation, the crowds in the streets, the pennants, and the flowers in the windows. The eminent Bacamarte, having entrusted her to the arm of Father Lopes, walked contemplatively with measured step. Dona Evarista, on the contrary, turned her head animatedly from side to side, observing with curiosity the unexpectedly warm reception. The priest asked about Rio de Janeiro, which he had not seen since the previous viceroyalty, and Dona Evarista replied that it was the most beautiful sight there could possibly be in the entire world. The Public Gardens, now completed, were a paradise in which she had often strolled—and the Street of Beautiful Nights, the Fountain of Ducks . . . Ah! the Fountain of Ducks. There really were ducks there, made of metal and spouting water through their mouths. A gorgeous thing. The priest said that Rio de Janeiro had been lovely even in his time there and must be much lovelier now. Small wonder, for it was so much larger than Itaguai and was, moreover, the capital. . . . But one could not call Itaguai ugly; it had some beautiful buildings, such as Mateus's mansion, the Green House . . .

"And apropos the Green House," said Father Lopes, gliding skillfully into the subject, "you will find it full of patients."

"Really?"

"Yes. Mateus is there. . . ."

"The saddler?"

"Costa is there too. So is Costa's cousin, and So-and-so, and What's-his-name, and . . ."

"All insane?"

"Apparently," replied the priest.

"But how? Why?"

Father Lopes drew down the corners of his mouth as if to say that he did not know or did not wish to tell what he knew—a vague reply, which could not be repeated to anyone. Dona Evarista found it strange indeed that all those people should have gone mad. It might easily happen to one or another—but to *all* of them? Yet she could hardly doubt the fact. Her husband was a learned man, a scientist; he would not commit anyone to the Green House without clear proof of insanity.

The priest punctuated her observations with an intermittent "undoubtedly . . . undoubtedly . . ."

A few hours later about fifty guests were seated at Simão Bacamarte's table for the home-coming dinner. Dona Evarista was the obligatory subject of toasts, speeches, and verses, all of them highly metaphorical. She was the wife of the new Hippocrates, the muse of science, an angel, the dawn, charity, consolation, life itself. Her eyes were two stars, according to Crispim

Soares, and two suns, by a Councilman's less modest figure. The
psychiatrist found all this a bit tiresome but showed no signs of
impatience. He merely leaned toward his wife and told her that
such flights of fancy, although permissible in rhetoric, were un-
substantiated in fact. Dona Evarista tried to accept this opinion;
but, even if she discounted three fourths of the flattery, there was
enough left to inflate her considerably. One of the orators, for
example—Martim Brito, twenty-five, a pretentious fop, much
addicted to women—declaimed that the birth of Dona Evarista
had come about in this manner: "After God gave the universe to
man and to woman, who are the diamond and the pearl of the
divine crown" (and the orator dragged this phrase triumphantly
from one end of the table to the other), "God decided to outdo
God and so he created Dona Evarista."

The psychiatrist's wife lowered her eyes with exemplary modesty. Two other ladies, who thought Martim Brito's expression
of adulation excessive and audacious, turned to observe its effect
on Dona Evarista's husband. They found his face clouded with
misgivings, threats, and possibly blood. The provocation was great
indeed, thought the two ladies. They prayed God to prevent any
tragic occurrence—or, better yet, to postpone it until the next
day. The more charitable of the two admitted (to herself) that
Dona Evarista was above suspicion, for she was so very unat-
tractive. And yet not all tastes were alike. Maybe some men . . .
This idea caused her to tremble again, although less violently
than before; less violently, for the psychiatrist was now smiling
at Martim Brito.

When everyone had risen from the table, Bacamarte walked
over to him and complimented him on his eulogy of Dona
Evarista. He said it was a brilliant improvisation, full of magnificent figures of speech. Had Brito himself originated the thought
about Dona Evarista's birth or had he taken it from something
he had read? No, it was entirely original; it had come to him as
he was speaking and he had considered it suitable for use as a
rhetorical climax. As a matter of fact, he always leaned toward
the bold and daring rather than the tender or jocose. He favored
the epic style. Once, for example, he had composed an ode on the
fall of the Marquis of Pombal in which he had said that "the foul
dragon of Nihility is crushed in the vengeful claws of the All."
And he had invented many other powerful figures of speech. He
liked sublime concepts, great and noble images. . . .

"Poor fellow!" thought the psychiatrist. "He's probably suffering from a cerebral lesion. Not a very serious case but worthy of study."

Three days later Dona Evarista learned, to her amazement, that Martim Brito was now living at the Green House. A young man with such beautiful thoughts! The two other ladies attributed his commitment to jealousy on the part of the psychiatrist, for the young man's words had been provocatively bold.

Jealousy? But how, then, can one explain the commitment a short time afterwards of persons of whom the doctor could not possibly have been jealous: innocuous, fun-loving Chico, Fabrício the notary, and many others. The terror grew in intensity. One no longer knew who was sane and who was insane. When their husbands went out in the street, the women of Itaguai lit candles to Our Lady. And some of the men hired bodyguards to go around with them.

Everyone who could possibly get out of town, did so. One of the fugitives, however, was seized just as he was leaving. He was Gil Bernardes, a friendly, polite young man; so polite, indeed, that he never said hello to anyone without doffing his hat and bowing to the ground. In the street he would sometimes run forty yards to shake the hand of a gentleman or lady—or even of a child, such as the Circuit Judge's little boy. He had a special talent for affability. He owed his acceptance by society not only to his personal charm but also to the noble tenacity with which he withstood any number of refusals, rejections, cold shoulders, and the like, without becoming discouraged. And, once he gained entry to a house, he never left it—nor did its occupants wish him to leave, for he was a delightful guest. Despite his popularity and the self-confidence it engendered, Gil Bernardes turned pale when he heard one day that the psychiatrist was watching him. The following morning he started to leave town but was apprehended and taken to the Green House.

"This must not be permitted to continue."

"Down with tyranny!"

"Despot! Outlaw! Goliath!"

At first such things were said softly and indoors. Later they were shouted in the streets. Rebellion was raising its ugly head. The thought of a petition to the government for the arrest and deportation of Simão Bacamarte occurred to many people even before Porfírio, with eloquent gestures of indignation expounded it in his barber shop. Let it be noted—and this is one of the finest pages of a somber history—that as soon as the population of the Green House began to grow so rapidly, Porfírio's profits also increased, for many of his customers now asked to be bled; but private interests, said the barber, have to yield to the public welfare. "The tyrant must be overthrown!" So great was his dedication to the cause that he uttered this cry shortly after he heard of the commitment of a man named Coelho who was bringing a lawsuit against him.

"How can anyone call Coelho crazy?" shouted Porfírio.

And no one answered. Everybody said he was perfectly sane. The legal action against the barber, involving some real estate, grew not out of hatred or spite but out of the obscure wording of a deed. Coelho had an excellent reputation. A few individuals, to be sure, avoided him; as soon as they saw him approaching in the distance they ran around corners, ducked into stores. The fact is, he loved conversation—long conversation, drunk down in large draughts. Consequently he was almost never alone. He preferred those who also liked to talk, but he would compromise, if necessary, for a unilateral conversation with the more taciturn. Whenever Father Lopes, who disliked Coelho, saw him taking his leave of someone, he quoted Dante, with a minor change of his own:

> "La bocca sollevò dal fiero pasto
> Quel seccatore . . ." *

But the priest's remark did not affect the general esteem in which Coelho was held, for some attributed the remark to mere personal animosity and others thought it was a prayer in Latin.

VI. The Rebellion

About thirty people allied themselves with the barber. They prepared a formal complaint and took it to the Town Council, which rejected it on the ground that scientific research must be

---

* "The pest raised his mouth from his savage repast." Father Lopes substituted *seccatore*, "pest," for Dante's *peccator*, "sinner." Count Ugolino, the sinner, was gnawing the head of another sinner. *Inferno*, Canto XXXIII.

hampered neither by hostile legislation nor by the misconceptions and prejudices of the mob.

"My advice to you," said the President of the Council, "is to disband and go back to work."

The group could hardly contain its anger. The barber declared that the people would march to the Green House and destroy it; that Itaguai must no longer be used as a corpse for dissection in the experiments of a medical despot; that several esteemed and even distinguished individuals, not to mention many humble but estimable persons, lay confined in the cubicles of the Green House; that the psychiatrist was clearly motivated by greed, for his compensation varied directly with the number of alleged madmen in his care—

"That's not true," interrupted the President.

"Not true?"

"About two weeks ago we received a communication from the illustrious doctor in which he stated that, in view of the great va▶to him as a scientist, of his observations and experiments, he would no longer accept payment from the Council or from the patients' families."

In view of this noble act of self-denial, how could the rebels persist in their attitude? The psychiatrist might, indeed, make mistakes, but obviously he was not motivated by any interest alien to science; and to establish error on his part, something more would be needed than disorderly crowds in the street. So spoke the President, and the entire Council applauded.

The barber meditated for a few moments and then declared that he was invested with a public mandate; he would give Itaguai no peace until the final destruction of the Green House, "that Bastille of human reason"—an expression he had heard a local poet use and which he now repeated with great vigor. Having spoken, he gave his cohorts a signal and led them out.

The Council was faced with an emergency. It must, at all costs, prevent rebellion and bloodshed. To make matters worse, one of the Councilmen who had supported the President was so impressed by the figure of speech, "Bastille of the human reason," that he changed his mind. He advocated adoption of a measure to liquidate the Green House. After the President had expressed his amazement and indignation, the dissenter observed:

"I know nothing about science, but if so many men whom we

considered sane are locked up as madmen, how do we know that
the real madman is not the psychiatrist himself?"

This Councilman, a highly articulate fellow named Sebastião
Freitas, spoke at some length. He presented the case against the
Green House with restraint but with firm conviction. His colleagues were dumbfounded. The President begged him at least
to help preserve law and order by not expressing his opinions in
the street, where they might give body and soul to what was so
far merely a whirlwind of uncoordinated atoms. This figure of
speech counterbalanced to some extent the one about the Bastille.
Sebastião Freitas promised to take no action for the present but
reserved the right to seek the elimination of the Green House by
legal means. And he murmured to himself lovingly: "That Bastille
of the human reason!"

Nevertheless, the crowd grew. Not thirty but three hundred
now followed the barber, whose nickname ought to be mentioned
at this point because it gave the rebellion its name: he was called
Stewed Corn, and the movement was therefore known ⬛lue.
Revolt of the Stewed Corners. Storming through the stree
ward the Green House, they might well have been compared to
the mob that stormed the Bastille, with due allowance, of course,
for the difference between Paris and Itaguaí.

A young child attached to the household ran in from the street
and told Dona Evarista the news. The psychiatrist's wife was
trying on a silk dress (one of the thirty-seven she had bought in
Rio).

"It's probably just a bunch of drunks," she said as she changed
the location of a pin. "Benedita, is the hem all right?"

"Yes, ma'am," replied the slave, who was squatting on the
floor, "it looks fine. Just turn a little bit. Like that. It's perfect,
ma'am."

"They're not a bunch of drunks, Dona Evarista," said the
child in fear. "They're shouting: 'Death to Dr. Bacamarte the
tyrant.'"

"Be quiet! Benedita, look over here on the left side. Don't
you think the seam is a little crooked? We'll have to rip it and
sew it again. Try to make it nice and even this time."

"Death to Dr. Bacamarte! Death to the tyrant!" howled three
hundred voices in the street.

The blood left Dona Evarista's face. She stood there like a

statue, petrified with terror. The slave ran instinctively to the back door. The child, whom Dona Evarista had refused to believe, enjoyed a moment of unexpressed but profound satisfaction. "Death to the psychiatrist!" shouted the voices, now closer than before.

Dona Evarista, although an easy prey to emotions of pleasure, was reasonably steadfast in adversity. She did not faint. She ran to the inside room where her husband was studying. At the moment of her precipitate entrance, the doctor was examining a passage in Averroës. His eyes, blind to external reality but highly perceptive in the realm of the inner life, rose from the book to the ceiling and returned to the book. Twice, Dona Evarista called him loudly by name without his paying her the least attention. The third time, he heard and asked what was troubling her.

"Can't you hear the shouting?"

The psychiatrist listened. The shouts were coming closer and closer, threatening, terrifying. He understood. Rising from the armchair, he shut the book and, with firm, calm step, walked over to the bookcase and put the volume back in its place. The insertion of the volume caused the books on either side of it to be slightly out of line. Simão Bacamarte carefully straightened them. Then he asked his wife to go to her room.

"No, no," begged his worthy helpmeet. "I want to die at your side where I belong."

Simão Bacamarte insisted that she go. He assured her that it was not a matter of life and death and told her that, even if it were, it would be her duty to remain alive. The unhappy lady bowed her head, tearful and obedient.

"Down with the Green House!" shouted the Stewed Corners.

The psychiatrist went out on the front balcony and faced the rebel mob, whose three hundred heads were radiant with civism and somber with fury. When they saw him they shouted: "Die! Die!" Simão Bacamarte indicated that he wished to speak, but they only shouted the louder. Then the barber waved his hat as a signal to his followers to be silent and told the psychiatrist that he might speak, provided his words did not abuse the patience of the people.

"I shall say little and, if possible, nothing at all. It depends on what it is that you have come to request."

"We aren't requesting anything," replied the barber, trembling with rage. "We are demanding that the Green House be destroyed or at least that all the prisoners in it be freed."

"I don't understand."

"You understand all right, tyrant. We want you to release the victims of your hatred, your whims, your greed. . . ."

The psychiatrist smiled, but the smile of this great man was not perceptible to the eyes of the multitude: it was a slight contraction of two or three muscles, nothing more.

"Gentlemen," he said, "science is a serious thing and it must be treated seriously. For my professional decisions I account to no one but God and the authorities in my special field. If you wish to suggest changes in the administration of the Green House, I am ready to listen to you; but if you wish me to be untrue to myself, further talk would be futile. I could invite you to appoint a committee to come and study the way I treat the madmen who have been committed to my care, but I shall not, for to do so would be to account to you for my methods and this I shall never do to a group of rebels or, for that matter, to laymen of any description."

So spoke the psychiatrist, and the people were astounded at his words. Obviously they had not expected such imperturbability and such resoluteness. Their amazement was even greater when the psychiatrist bowed gravely to them, turned his back, and walked slowly back into the house. The barber soon regained his self-possession and, waving his hat, urged the mob to demolish the Green House. The voices that took up the cry were few and weak. At this decisive moment the barber felt a surging ambition to rule. If he succeeded in overthrowing the psychiatrist and destroying the Green House, he might well take over the Town Council, dominate the other municipal authorities, and make himself the master of Itaguai. For some years now he had striven to have his name included in the ballots from which the Councilmen were selected by lot, but his petitions were denied because his position in society was considered incompatible with such a responsibility. It was a case of now or never. Besides, he had carried the street riot to such a point that defeat would mean prison and perhaps banishment or even the scaffold. Unfortunately, the psychiatrist's reply had taken most of the steam out of the Stewed Corners. When the barber perceived this, he felt like shouting: "Wretches! Cowards!" But he contained himself and merely said:

"My friends, let us fight to the end! The salvation of Itaguai is in your worthy and heroic hands. Let us destroy the foul prison that confines or threatens your children and parents, your mothers and sisters, your relatives and friends, and you yourselves. Do you want to be thrown into a dungeon and starved on bread and water or maybe whipped to death?"

The mob bestirred itself, murmured, shouted, and gathered around the barber. The revolt was emerging from its stupor and threatening to demolish the Green House.

"Come on!" shouted Porfírio, waving his hat.

"Come on!" echoed his followers.

At that moment a corps of dragoons turned the corner and came marching toward the mob.

VII. The Unexpected

The mob appeared stupefied by the arrival of the dragoons; the Stewed Corners could hardly believe that the force of the law was being exerted against them. The dragoons halted and their captain ordered the crowd to disperse. Some of the rebels felt inclined to obey, but others rallied around the barber, who boldly replied to the captain:

"We shall not disperse. If you wish, you may take our lives, but nothing else: we will not yield our honor or our rights, for on them depends the salvation of Itaguai."

Nothing could have been more imprudent or more natural than this reply. It reflected the ecstasy inspired by great crises. Perhaps it reflected also an excess of confidence in the captain's forbearance, a confidence soon dispelled by the captain's order to charge. What followed is indescribable. The mob howled its fury. Some managed to escape by climbing into windows or running down the street, but the majority, inspired by the barber's words, snorted with anger and stood their ground. The defeat of the Stewed Corners appeared imminent, when suddenly one third of the dragoons, for reasons not set forth in the chronicles, went over to the side of the rebels. This unexpected reënforcement naturally heartened the Stewed Corners and discouraged the ranks of legality. The loyal soldiers refused to attack their comrades and, one by one, joined them, with the result that in a few minutes the entire aspect of the struggle had changed. The captain, defended by only a handful of his men against a compact mass of rebels and soldiers, gave up and surrendered his sword to the barber.

The triumphant rebels did not lose an instant. They carried the wounded into the nearest houses and headed for the town hall. The people and the troops fraternized. They shouted *vivas* for the King, the Viceroy, Itaguai, and "our great leader, Porfírio." The barber marched at their head, wielding the sword as dexterously as if it had been merely an unusually long razor. Victory hovered like a halo above him, and the dignity of government informed his every movement.

The Councilmen, watching from the windows, thought that the troops had captured the Stewed Corners. The Council formally resolved to send a petition to the Viceroy asking him to give an extra month's pay to the dragoons, "whose high devotion to duty has saved Itaguai from the chaos of rebellion and mob rule." This phrase was proposed by Sebastião Freitas, whose defense of the rebels had so scandalized his colleagues. But the legislators were soon disillusioned. They could now clearly hear the *vivas* for the barber and the shouts of "death to the Councilmen" and "death to the psychiatrist." The President held his head high and said: "Whatever may be our fate, let us never forget that we are the servants of His Majesty and of the people of Itaguai." Sebastião suggested that perhaps they could best serve the Crown and the town by sneaking out the back door and going to the Circuit Judge's office for advice and help, but all the other members of the Council rejected this suggestion.

A few seconds later the barber and some of his lieutenants entered the chamber and told the Town Council that it had been deposed. The Councilmen surrendered and were put in jail. Then the barber's friends urged him to assume the dictatorship of Itaguai in the name of His Majesty. Porfírio accepted this responsibility, although, as he told them, he was fully aware of its weight and of the thorny problems it entailed. He said also that he would be unable to rule without their coöperation, which they promptly promised him. The barber then went to the window and told the people what had happened; they shouted their approval. He chose the title, "Town Protector in the Name of His Majesty and of the People." He immediately issued several important orders, official communications from the new government, a detailed statement to the Viceroy with many protestations of obedience to His Majesty, and finally the following short but forceful proclamation to the people:

Fellow Itaguaians:

A corrupt and irresponsible Town Council was conspiring ignominiously against His Majesty and against the people. Public opinion had condemned it, and now a handful of citizens, with the help of His Majesty's brave dragoons, have dissolved it. By unanimous consent I am empowered to rule until His Majesty chooses to take formal action in the premises. Itaguaians, I ask only for your trust and for your help in restoring peace and the public funds, recklessly squandered by the Council. You may count on me to make every personal sacrifice for the common good, and you may rest assured that we shall have the full support of the Crown.

Porfírio Caetano das Neves
Town Protector in the Name of His Majesty and of the People

Everyone remarked that the proclamation said nothing whatever about the Green House, and some considered this ominous. The danger seemed all the greater when, in the midst of the important changes that were taking place, the psychiatrist committed to the Green House some seven or eight new patients, including a relative of the Protector. Everybody erroneously interpreted Bacamarte's action as a challenge to the barber and thought it likely that within twenty-four hours the terrible prison would be destroyed and the psychiatrist would be in chains.

The day ended happily. While the crier with the noisemaker went from corner to corner reading the proclamation, the people walked about the streets and swore they would be willing to die for the Protector. There were very few shouts of opposition to the Green House, for the people were confident that the government would soon liquidate it. Porfírio declared the day an official holiday and, to promote an alliance between the temporal power and the spiritual power, he asked Father Lopes to celebrate the occasion with a Te Deum. The Vicar issued a public refusal.

"May I at least assume," asked the barber with a threatening frown, "that you will not ally yourself with the enemies of the government?"

"How can I ally myself with your enemies," replied Father Lopes (if one can call it a reply), "when you have no enemies? You say in your proclamation that you are ruling by unanimous consent."

The barber could not help smiling. He really had almost no opposition. Apart from the captain of dragoons, the Council, and some of the town bigwigs, everybody acclaimed him; and even the bigwigs did not actually oppose him. Indeed, the people blessed the name of the man who would finally free Itaguai from the Green House and from the terrible Simão Bacamarte.

VIII. The Druggist's Dilemma

The next day Porfírio and two of his aides-de-camp left the government palace (the new name of the town hall) and set out for the residence of Simão Bacamarte. The barber knew that it would have been more fitting for him to have ordered Bacamarte to come to the palace, but he was afaid the psychiatrist would refuse and so he decided to exercise forbearance in the use of his powers.

Crispim Soares was in bed at the time. The druggist was undergoing continual mental torture these days. His intimacy with Simão Bacamarte called him to the doctor's defense, and Porfírio's victory called him to the barber's side. This victory, together with the intensity of the hatred for Bacamarte, made it unprofitable and perhaps dangerous for Crispim to continue to associate with the doctor. But the druggist's wife, a masculine woman who was very close to Dona Evarista, told him that he owed the psychiatrist an obligation of loyalty. The dilemma appeared insoluble, so Crispim avoided it by the only means he could devise: he said he was sick, and went to bed.

The next day his wife told him that Porfírio and some other men were headed for Simão Bacamarte's house.

"They're going to arrest him," thought the druggist.

One idea led to another. He imagined that their next step would be to arrest him, Crispim Soares, as an accessory. The therapeutic effect of this thought was remarkable. The druggist jumped out of bed and, despite his wife's protests, dressed and went out. The chroniclers all agree that Mrs. Soares found great comfort in the nobility of her husband, who, she assumed, was going to the defense of his friend, and they note with perspicacity the immense power of a thought, even if untrue; for the druggist walked not to the house of the psychiatrist but straight to the government palace. When he got there he expressed disappointment that the barber was out; he had wanted to assure him of his loyalty and support. Indeed, he had intended to do this the day before but had been prevented by illness—an illness that he now evidenced by a forced cough. The high officials to whom he spoke knew of his intimacy with the psychiatrist and therefore appreciated the significance of this declaration of loyalty. They treated the druggist with the greatest respect. They told him that the Protector had gone to the Green House on important business but would soon return. They offered him a chair, refreshments, and flattery. They told him that the cause of the illustrious Porfírio was the cause of every true patriot—a proposition with which Crispim Soares heartily agreed and which he proposed to affirm in a vigorous communication to the Viceroy.

IX. Two Beautiful Cases

The psychiatrist received the barber immediately. He told him that he had no means of resistance and was therefore prepared to submit to the new government. He asked only that they not force him to be present at the destruction of the Green House.

"The doctor is under a misapprehension," said Porfírio after a pause. "We are not vandals. Rightly or wrongly, everybody thinks that most of the people locked up here are perfectly sane. But the government recognizes that the question is purely scientific and that scientific issues cannot be resolved by legislation. Moreover, the Green House is now an established municipal institution. We must therefore find a compromise that will both permit its continued operation and placate the public."

The psychiatrist could not conceal his amazement. He confessed that he had expected not only destruction of the Green

House but also his own arrest and banishment. The last thing in the world he would have expected was—

"That is because you don't appreciate the grave responsibility of government," interrupted the barber. "The people, in their blindness, may feel righteous indignation about something that they do not understand; they have a right, then, to ask the government to act along certain lines. The government, however, must remember its duty to promote the public interest, whether or not this interest is in full accord with the demands made by the public itself. The revolution, which yesterday overthrew a corrupt and despicable Town Council, screams for destruction of the Green House. But the government must remain calm and objective. It knows that elimination of the Green House would not eliminate insanity. It knows that the mentally ill must receive treatment. It knows also that it cannot itself provide this treatment and that it even lacks the ability to distinguish the sane from the insane. These are matters for science, not for politics. They are matters requiring the sort of delicate, trained judgment that you, not we, are fitted to exercise. All I ask is that you help me give some degree of satisfaction to the people of Itaguai. If you and the government present a united front and propose a compromise of some sort, the people will accept it. Let me suggest, unless you have something better to propose, that we free those patients who are practically cured and those whose illnesses are relatively mild. In this way we can show how benign and generous we are without seriously handicapping your work."

Simão Bacamarte remained silent for about three minutes and then asked: "How many casualties were there in the fighting yesterday?"

The barber thought the question a little odd, but quickly replied that eleven had been killed and twenty-five wounded.

"Eleven dead, twenty-five wounded," repeated the psychiatrist two or three times.

Then he said that he did not like the barber's suggestion and that he would try to devise a better compromise, which he would communicate to the government within a few days. He asked a number of questions about the events of the day before: the attack by the dragoons, the defense, the change of sides by the dragoons, the Council's resistance, and so on. The barber replied in detail, with emphasis on the discredit into which the Council had fallen. He admitted that the government did not yet have the support of the most important men in the community and added that the psychiatrist might be very helpful in this connection. The government would be pleased, indeed, if it could count among its friends the loftiest spirit in Itaguai and, doubtless, in the entire kingdom. Nothing that the barber said, however, changed the expression on the doctor's austere face. Bacamarte evidenced neither vanity nor modesty; he listened in silence, as impassive as a stone god.

"Eleven dead, twenty-five wounded," repeated the psychiatrist after the visitors had left. "Two beautiful cases. This barber shows unmistakable symptoms of psychopathic duplicity. As for proof of the insanity of the people who acclaim him, what more could one ask than the fact that eleven were killed and twenty-five wounded? Two beautiful cases!"

"Long live our glorious Protector!" shouted thirty-odd people who had been awaiting the barber in front of the house.

The psychiatrist went to the window and heard part of the barber's speech:

". . . for my main concern, day and night, is to execute faithfully the will of the people. Trust in me and you will not be disappointed. I ask of you only one thing: be peaceful, maintain order. For order, my friends, is the foundation on which government must rest."

"Long live Porfírio!" shouted the people, waving their hats.

"Two beautiful cases," murmured the psychiatrist.

X. The Restoration

Within a week there were fifty additional patients in the Green House, all of them strong supporters of the new government. The people felt outraged. The government was stunned; it did not know how to react. João Pina, another barber, said openly that Porfírio had "sold his birthright to Simão Bacamarte for a pot of gold"—a phrase that attracted some of the more indignant citizens to Pina's side. Porfírio, seeing his competitor at the head of a potential insurrection, knew that he would be overthrown if he did not immediately change his course. He therefore issued two decrees, one abolishing the Green House and the other banishing the psychiatrist from Itaguai.

João Pina, however, explained clearly and eloquently that these decrees were a hoax, a mere face-saving gesture. Two hours later Porfírio was deposed and João Pina assumed the heavy burden of government. Pina found copies of the proclamation to the people, the explanatory statement to the Viceroy, and other documents issued by his predecessor. He had new originals made and sent them out over his own name and signature. The chronicles note that the wording of the new documents was a little different. For example, where the other barber had spoken of "a corrupt and irresponsible Town Council," João Pina spoke of "a body contaminated by French doctrines wholly contrary to the sacrosanct interests of His Majesty."

The new dictator barely had time to dispatch the documents when a military force sent by the Viceroy entered the town and restored order. At the psychiatrist's request, the troops immediately handed over to him Porfírio and some fifty other persons, and promised to deliver seventeen more of the barber's followers as soon as they had sufficiently recovered from their wounds.

This period in the crisis of Itaguai represents the culmination of Simão Bacamarte's influence. He got whatever he wanted. For example, the Town Council, now reëstablished, promptly consented to have Sebastião Freitas committed to the asylum. The psychiatrist had requested this in view of the extraordinary inconsistency of the Councilman's opinions, which Bacamarte considered a clear sign of mental illness. Subsequently the same thing happened to Crispim Soares. When the psychiatrist learned that his close friend and staunch supporter had suddenly gone over to the side of the Stewed Corners, he ordered him to be seized and taken to the Green House. The druggist did not deny his switch of allegiance but explained that he had been motivated by an overwhelming fear of the new government. Simão Bacamarte accepted the explanation as true; he pointed out, however, that fear is a common symptom of mental abnormality.

Perhaps the most striking proof of the psychiatrist's influence was the docility with which the Town Council surrendered to him its own President. This worthy official had declared that the affront to the Council could be washed away only by the blood of the Stewed Corners. Bacamarte learned of this through the Secretary of the Council, who repeated the President's words with immense enthusiasm. The psychiatrist first committed the Secretary to the Green House and then proceeded to the town hall. He told the Council that its President was suffering from hemoferal mania, an illness that he planned to study in depth, with, he hoped, immense benefit to the world. The Council hesitated for a moment and then acquiesced.

From that day on, the population of the asylum increased even more rapidly than before. A person could not utter the most commonplace lie, even a lie that clearly benefited him, without being immediately committed to the Green House. Scandal-mongers, dandies, people who spent hours at puzzles, people who habitually inquired into the private lives of others, officials puffed up with authority—the psychiatrist's agents brought them all in. He spared sweethearts but not flirts, for he maintained that the former obeyed a healthful impulse, but that the latter yielded to a morbid desire for conquest. He discriminated against neither the avaricious nor the prodigal: both were committed to the asylum; this led people to say that the psychiatrist's concept of madness included practically everybody.

Some of the chroniclers express doubts about Simão Baca-marte's integrity. They note that, at his instigation, the Town Council authorized all persons who boasted of noble blood to wear a silver ring on the thumb of the left hand. These chroniclers point out that, as a consequence of the ordinance, a jeweler who was a close friend of Bacamarte became rich. Another conse-quence, however, was the commitment of the ring-wearers to the Green House; and the treatment of these unfortunate people, rather than the enrichment of his friend, may well have been the objective of the illustrious physician. Nobody was sure what conduct on the part of the ring-wearers had betrayed their ill-ness. Some thought it was their tendency to gesticulate a great deal, especially with the left hand, no matter where they were— at home, in the street, even in church. Everybody knows that madmen gesticulate a great deal.

"Where will this man stop?" said the important people of the town. "Ah, if only we had supported the Stewed Corners!"

One day, when preparations were being made for a ball to be held that evening in the town hall, Itaguai was shocked to hear that Simão Bacarmarte had sent his own wife to the asylum. At first everyone thought it was a gag of some sort. But it was the absolute truth. Dona Evarista had been committed at two o'clock in the morning.

"I had long suspected that she was a sick woman," said the psychiatrist in response to a question from Father Lopes. "Her moderation in all other matters was hard to reconcile with her mania for silks, velvets, laces, and jewelry, a mania that began immediately after her return from Rio de Janeiro. It was then that I started to observe her closely. Her conversation was always about these objects. If I talked to her about the royal courts of earlier times, she wanted to know what kind of clothes the women wore. If a lady visited her while I was out, the first thing my wife told me, even before mentioning the purpose of the visit, was how the woman was dressed and which jewels or articles of clothing were pretty and which were ugly. Once (I think Your Reverence will remember this) she said she was going to make a new dress every year for Our Lady of the Mother Church. All these symptoms indicated a serious condition. Tonight, however, the full gravity of her illness became manifest. She had selected the entire outfit she would wear to the ball and had it all fixed and ready. All except one thing: she couldn't decide between a garnet necklace and a sapphire necklace. The day before yesterday she asked me which she should wear. I told her it didn't matter, that they both were very becoming. Yesterday at lunch she repeated the question. After dinner she was silent and pensive. I asked her what was the matter. 'I want to wear my beautiful garnet necklace, but my sapphire one is so lovely.' 'Then wear the sapphire necklace.' 'But then I can't wear the garnet necklace.' In the middle of the night, about half-past one, I awoke. She was not in bed. I got up and went to the dressing-room. There she sat with the two necklaces, in front of the mirror, trying on first one and then the other. An obvious case of dementia. I had her put away immediately."

Father Lopes said nothing. The explanation did not wholly satisfy him. Perceiving this, the psychiatrist told him that the specific illness of Dona Evarista was vestimania; it was by no means incurable.

"I hope to have her well within two weeks and, in any event,

I expect to learn a great deal from the study of her case," said the psychiatrist in conclusion.

This personal sacrifice greatly enhanced the public image of the illustrious doctor. Suspicion, distrust, accusations were all negated by the commitment of his own wife whom he loved with all his heart. No one could ever again charge him with motives other than those of science itself. He was beyond doubt a man of integrity and profound objectivity, a combination of Cato and Hippocrates.

XI. Release and Joy

And now let the reader share with the people of Itaguai their amazement on learning one day that the madmen of the Green House had been released.

"All of them?"

"All of them."

"Impossible. Some, maybe. But all?"

"All. He said so himself in a communiqué that he sent today to the Town Council."

The psychiatrist informed the Council, first, that he had checked the statistics and had found that four-fifths of the population of Itaguai was in the Green House; second, that this disproportionately large number of patients had led him to reëxamine his fundamental theory of mental illness, a theory that classified as sick all people who were mentally unbalanced; third, that as a consequence of this reëxamination in the light of the statistics, he had concluded not only that his theory was unsound but also that the exactly contrary doctrine was true—that is, that normality lay in a lack of equilibrium and that the abnormal, the really sick, were the well balanced, the thoroughly rational; fourth, that in view of the foregoing he would release the persons now confined and would commit to the Green House all persons found to be mentally ill under the new theory; fifth, that he would continue to devote himself to the pursuit of scientific truth and trusted that the Council would continue to give him its support; and sixth, that he would give back the funds he had received for the board and lodging of the patients, less the amounts already expended, which could be verified by examination of his records and accounts.

The amazement of Itaguai was no greater than the joy of the relatives and friends of the former patients. Dinners, dances, Chinese lanterns, music, everything to celebrate the happy occasion. I shall not describe the festivities, for they are merely peripheral to this history; suffice it to say that they were elaborate, long, and memorable.

In the midst of all this rejoicing, nobody noticed the last part of the fourth item in the psychiatrist's communiqué.

XII. The Last Part of the Fourth Item

The lanterns were taken down, the ex-patients resumed their former lives, everything appeared normal. Councilman Freitas and the President returned to their accustomed places, and the Council governed Itaguai without external interference. Porfírio the barber had "experienced everything," as the poet said of Napoleon; indeed, Porfírio had experienced more than Napoleon, for Napoleon was never committed to the Green House. The barber now found the obscure security of his trade preferable to the brilliant calamities of power. He was tried for his crimes and convicted, but the people begged His Majesty to pardon their ex-Protector, and His Majesty did so. The authorities decided not to prosecute João Pina, for he had overthrown an unlawful ruler. The chroniclers maintain that Pina's absolution inspired our adage:

> A judge will never throw the book
> At crook who steals from other crook.

An immoral adage, but immensely useful.

There were no more complaints against the psychiatrist. There was not even resentment for his past acts. Indeed, the former patients were grateful because he had declared them sane; they gave a ball in his honor. The chroniclers relate that Dona Evarista decided at first to leave her husband but changed her mind when she contemplated the emptiness of a life without him. Her devotion to this high-minded man overcame her wounded vanity, and they lived together more happily than ever before.

On the basis of the new psychiatric doctrine set forth in the communiqué, Crispim Soares concluded that his prudence in allying himself with the revolution had been a manifestation of mental health. He was deeply touched by Bacamarte's magnanimity: the psychiatrist had extended his hand to his old friend upon releasing him from the Green House.

"A great man," said the druggist to his wife.

We need not specifically note the release of Costa, Coelho, and the other patients named in this history. Each was now free to resume his previous way of life. Martim Brito, for example, who had been committed because of a speech in excessive praise of Dona Evarista, now made another in honor of the doctor, "whose exalted genius lifted its wings and flew far above the common herd until it rivaled the sun in altitude and in brilliance."

"Thank you," said the psychiatrist. "Obviously I was right to set you free."

Meanwhile, the Town Council passed, without debate, an ordinance to take care of the last part of the fourth item in Bacamarte's communiqué. The ordinance authorized the psychiatrist to commit to the Green House all persons whom he found to be mentally well balanced. But, remembering its painful experience in connection with public reaction to the asylum, the Council added a proviso in which it stated that, since the purpose of the ordinance was to provide an opportunity for the doctor to test his new theory, the authorization would remain in effect for only one year, and the Council reserved the right to close the asylum at any time if the maintenance of public order so required.

Sebastião Freitas proposed an amendment to the effect that under no circumstances were members of the Council to be committed to the Green House. The amendment was adopted almost unanimously. The only dissenting vote was cast by Councilman Galvão. He argued calmly that, in authorizing a scientific experiment on the people of Itaguai, the Council would itself be unscientific if it exempted its members or any other segment of the population from subjection to the experiment. "Our public office," he said, "does not exclude us from the human race." But he was shouted down.

Simão Bacamarte accepted the ordinance with all its restrictions. As for the exemption of the Councilmen, he declared that they were in no danger whatever of being committed, for their votes in favor of the amendment showed clearly that they were mentally unbalanced. He asked only that Galvão be delivered to him, for this Councilman had exhibited exceptional mental equilibrium, not only in his objection to the amendment but even more in the calm that he had maintained in the face of unreasonable opposition and abuse on the part of his colleagues. The Council immediately granted the request.

Under the new theory a few acts or statements by a person could not establish his abnormality: a long examination and a thorough study of his history were necessary. Father Lopes, for example, was not taken to the Green House until thirty days after the passage of the ordinance. In the case of the druggist's wife fifty days of study were required. Crispim Soares raged about the streets, telling everybody that he would tear the tyrant's ears off. One of the men to whom he spoke—a fellow who, as everyone knew, had an aversion for Bacamarte—ran and warned the psychiatrist. Bacamarte thanked him warmly and locked him up in recognition of his rectitude and his good will even toward someone he disliked, signs of perfect mental equilibrium.

"This is a very unusual case," said the doctor to Dona Evarista.

By the time Crispim Soares arrived at the psychiatrist's house, sorrow had overcome his anger. He did not tear Bacamarte's ears off. The psychiatrist tried to comfort his old friend. He told him that his wife might be suffering from a cerebral lesion, that there was a fair chance of recovery, and that meanwhile he must of course keep her confined. The psychiatrist considered it desirable, however, for Soares to spend a good deal of time with her, for the druggist's guile and intellectual dishonesty might help to overcome the moral superiority that the doctor found in his patient.

"There is no reason," he said, "why you and your wife should not eat lunch and dinner together every day at the Green House. You may even stay with her at night."

Simão Bacamarte's words placed the druggist in a new dilemma. He wanted to be with his wife, but at the same time he dreaded returning to the Green House. He remained undecided for several minutes. Then Dona Evarista released him from the dilemma: she promised to visit his wife frequently and to bear messages between the two. Crispim Soares kissed her hands in gratitude. His pusillanimous egoism struck the psychiatrist as almost sublime.

Although it took Bacamarte almost half a year to find eighteen patients for the Green House, he did not relax his efforts to discover the insane. He went from street to street, from house to house, observing, inquiring, taking notes. And when he committed someone to the asylum, it was with the same sense of accomplishment with which he had formerly committed dozens at a time. This very disproportion confirmed his new theory. At last the truth about mental illness was definitely known. One day Bacamarte committed the Circuit Judge to the Green House, after weeks of detailed 'study of the man's acts and thorough interrogation of his friends, who included all the important people of Itaguaí.

More than once the psychiatrist was on the point of sending someone to the Green House, only to discover a serious shortcoming at the last moment. In the case of the lawyer Salustiano, for example, he thought he had found so perfect a combination of intellectual and moral qualities that it would be dangerous to leave the man at large. He told one of his agents to bring the man in, but the agent, who had known many lawyers, suspected that he might really be sane and persuaded Bacamarte to authorize a little experiment. The agent had a close friend who was charged with having falsified a will. He advised this friend to engage Salustiano as his lawyer.

"Do you really think he'll take the case?"

"Sure he will. Confess everything to him. He'll get you off."

The agent's friend went to the lawyer, admitted that he had falsified the will, and begged him to accept the case. Salustiano did not turn the man away. He studied the charges and supporting evidence. In court he argued at great length, proving conclusively that the will was genuine. After a verdict of acquittal the defendant received the estate under the terms of the will. To this experiment both he and the learned counselor owed their freedom.

Very little escapes the comprehension of a man of genuine insight. For some time Simão Bacamarte had noted the wisdom, patience, and dedication of the agent who devised the experiment. Consequently he determined to commit him to the Green House, in which he gave him one of the choicest cubicles.

The patients were segregated into classes. In one gallery lived only those whose outstanding moral quality was modesty. The notably tolerant occupied another gallery, and still others were set aside for the truthful, the guileless, the loyal, the magnanimous, the wise. Naturally, the friends and relatives of the madmen railed against the new theory. Some even tried to persuade the Town Council to cancel the authorization it had given Bacamarte. The Councilmen, however, remembered with bitterness the word of their former colleague Galvão; they did not wish to see him back in their midst, and so they refused. Simão Bacamarte sent a message to the Council, not thanking it but congratulating it on this act of personal spite.

Some of the important people of Itaguai then went secretly to the barber Porfírio. They promised to support him with men, money, and influence if he would lead another movement against the psychiatrist and the Town Council. He replied that ambition had once led him to violent transgression of the law but that he now recognized the folly of such conduct; that the Council, in its wisdom, had authorized the psychiatrist to conduct his new experiment for a year; that anybody who objected should wait till the end of the year and then, if the Council insisted on renewing the authorization, should petition the Viceroy; that he would not recommend recourse again to a method that had done no good and had caused several deaths and other casualties, which would be an eternal burden on his conscience.

The psychiatrist listened with immense interest when one of his secret agents told him what Porfírio had said. Two days later the barber was locked up in the Green House. "You're damned if you do and you're damned if you don't," observed the new patient.

At the end of the year allowed for verification of the new theory, the Town Council authorized the psychiatrist to continue his work for another six months in order to experiment with methods of therapy. The result of this additional experimentation is so significant that it merits ten chapters, but I shall content myself with one. It will provide the reader with an inspiring example of scientific objectivity and selflessness.

XIII. Plus Ultra

However diligent and perceptive he may have been in the discovery of madmen, Simão Bacamarte outdid himself when he undertook to cure them. All the chroniclers agree that he brought about the most amazing recoveries.

It is indeed hard to imagine a more rational system of therapy. Having divided the patients into classes according to their predominant moral qualities, the doctor now proceeded to break down those qualities. He applied a remedy in each case to inculcate exactly the opposite characteristic, selecting the specific medicine and dose best suited to the patient's age, personality, and social position.

The cases of modesty may serve as examples. In some, a wig, a fine coat, or a cane would suffice to restore reason to the madman. In more difficult cases the psychiatrist resorted to diamonds, honorary degrees, and the like. The illness of one modest lunatic, a poet, resisted every sort of therapy. Bacamarte had almost given up, when an idea occurred to him: he would have the crier with the noisemaker proclaim the patient to be as great as Garção or Pindar.

"It was like a miracle," said the poet's mother to one of her friends. "My boy is entirely well now. A miracle . . ."

Another patient, also in the modest class, seemed incurable. The specific remedy used for the poet would not work, for this patient was not a writer; indeed, he could barely sign his name. But Dr. Bacamarte proved equal to the challenge. He decided to have the patient made Secretary to the Itaguai branch of the Royal Academy. The Secretary and the President of each branch were appointed by the Crown. They enjoyed the privileges of being addressed as Excellency and of wearing a gold medallion. The government at Lisbon refused Bacamarte's request at first; but after the psychiatrist explained that he did not ask the appointment as a real honor for his patient but merely as a therapeutic device to cure a difficult case, and after the Minister of Overseas Possessions (a cousin of the patient) intervened, the government finally granted the request. The consequent cure was hailed as another miracle.

"Wonderful, really wonderful!" said everybody upon seeing the healthy, prideful expression on the faces of the two ex-madmen.

Bacamarte's method was ultimately successful in every case, although in a few the patient's dominant quality proved impregnable. In these cases the psychiatrist won out by attacking at another point, like a good military strategist.

By the end of five months all the patients had been cured. The Green House was empty. Councilman Galvão, so cruelly afflicted with fairness and moderation, had the good fortune to lose an uncle; I say good fortune, for the uncle's will was ambiguous and Galvão obtained a favorable interpretation of it by bribing two judges. With customary integrity, the doctor admitted that the cure had been effected not by him but by nature's *vis medicatrix*. It was quite otherwise in the case of Father Lopes. Bacamarte knew that the priest was utterly ignorant of Greek, and therefore asked him to make a critical analysis of the Septuagint. Father Lopes accepted the task. In two months he had written a book on the subject and was released from the Green House. As for the druggist's wife, she remained there only a short time.

"Why doesn't Crispim come to visit me?" she asked every day.

They gave her various answers and finally told her the plain truth. The worthy matron could not contain her shame and indignation. Her explosions of wrath included such expressions as "rat," "coward," and "he even cheats on prescriptions." Simão Bacamarte remarked that, whether or not these characterizations of her husband were true, they clearly established the lady's return to sanity. He promptly released her.

If you think the psychiatrist was radiant with happiness on seeing the last guest leave the Green House, you apparently do not yet understand the man. *Plus ultra* was his motto. For him the discovery of the true theory of mental illness was not enough, nor was the establishment in Itaguai of the reign of reason with the total elimination of psychological abnormality. *Plus ultra!* Something told him that his new theory bore within itself a better, newer theory.

"Let us see," he said to himself, "if I can discover the ultimate, underlying truth."

He paced the length of the immense room, past bookcase after bookcase—the largest library in His Majesty's overseas possessions. A gold-embroidered, damask dressing-gown (a gift from a university) enveloped the regal and austere body of the illustrious physician. The extensive top of his head, which the incessant cogitations of the scientist had rendered bald, was covered by a wig. His feet, neither dainty nor gross but perfectly proportioned to his body, were encased in a pair of ordinary shoes with plain brass buckles. Note the distinction: only those elements that bore some relationship to his work as a scientist were in any sense luxurious; the rest was simple and temperate.

And so the psychiatrist walked up and down his vast library, lost in thought, alien to everything but the dark problem of psychopathology. Suddenly he stopped. Standing before a window, with his left elbow resting on his open right hand and his chin on his closed left hand, he asked himself:

"Were they all really insane? Did I really cure them? Or is not mental imbalance so natural and inherent that it was bound to assert itself with or without my help?"

He soon arrived at this conclusion: the apparently well-balanced minds that he had just "cured" had really been unbalanced all the time, just like the obviously sane minds of the rest of the people. Their apparent illness was superficial and transient.

The psychiatrist contemplated his new doctrine with mixed feelings. He was happy because, after such long study, experimentation, and struggle, he could at last affirm the ultimate truth: there never were and never would be any madmen in Itaguai or anywhere else. But he was unhappy because a doubt assailed him. In the field of psychiatry a generalization so broad, so absolute, was almost inevitably erroneous. If he could find just one undeniably well balanced, virtuous, insane man, the new theory would be acceptable—not as an absolute, exceptionless principle, which was inadmissible, but as a general rule applicable to all but the most extraordinary cases.

According to the chroniclers, this difficulty constituted the most dreadful of the spiritual tempests through which the courageous Bacamarte passed in the course of his stormy professional life. But tempests terrify only the weak. After twenty minutes a gentle but radiant dawn dispelled the darkness from the face of the psychiatrist.

"Of course. That's it, of course."

What Simão Bacamarte meant was that he had found in himself the perfect, undeniable case of insanity. He possessed wisdom, patience, tolerance, truthfulness, loyalty, and moral fortitude—all the qualities that go to make an utter madman.

But then he questioned his own self-observation. Surely he must be imperfect in some way. To ascertain the truth about himself he convoked a gathering of his friends and questioned them. He begged them to answer with absolute frankness. They all agreed that he had not been mistaken.

"No defects?"

"None at all," they replied in chorus.

"No vices?"

"None."

"Perfect in every respect?"

"In every respect."

"No, impossible!" cried the psychiatrist. "I cannot believe that I am so far superior to my fellow men. You are letting yourselves be influenced by your affection for me."

His friends insisted. The psychiatrist hesitated, but Father Lopes made it difficult for him not to accept their judgment.

"Do you know why you are reluctant to recognize in yourself the lofty qualities which we all see so clearly?" said the priest. "It is because you have an additional quality that enhances all the others: modesty."

Simão Bacamarte bowed his head. He was both sad and happy, but more happy than sad. He immediately committed himself to the Green House. His wife and his friends begged him not to. They told him he was perfectly sane. They wept, they pleaded. All in vain.

"This is a matter of science, of a new doctrine," he said, "and I am the first instance of its application. I embody both theory and practice."

"Simão! Simão, my love!" cried his wife. Her face was bathed in tears.

But the doctor, his eyes alight with scientific conviction, gently pushed her away. He entered the Green House, shut the door behind him, and set about the business of curing himself. The chroniclers state, however, that he died seventeen months later as insane as ever. Some even venture the opinion that he was the only madman (in the vulgar or non-Bacamartian sense) ever committed to the asylum. But this opinion should not be taken seriously. It was based on remarks attributed to Father Lopes—doubtless erroneously, for, as everybody knew, the priest liked and admired the psychiatrist. In any case, the people of Itaguai buried the mortal remains of Simão Bacamarte with great pomp and solemnity.

Translated by WILLIAM L. GROSSMAN

A Woman's Arms

Ignacio quailed before the lawyer's yelling, took the plate he handed him, and began to eat under a thunderclap of names: loafer, blockhead, stupid, crazy . . .

"Where are your thoughts that you never hear what I say to you? I'm going to tell your father and let him shake the laziness out of you with a quince rod or a good big stick. You're not too old to get a whipping, and don't you ever think you are. Stupid, crazy! . . .

"And outside it's just what you see here at home," he went on, turning to Dona Severina, a lady who had lived with him, maritally that is, for a number of years. "He gets my papers all mixed up, goes to the wrong address, calls on one court stenographer instead of another, switches attorneys on me: it's the very devil! He goes around asleep all the time. Look at him in the morning —you have to break his bones to get him out of bed . . . Just wait! Tomorrow I'll wake him up with a broom handle!"

Dona Severina touched his foot as if begging him to stop. Borges spit out a few more abusive observations, and was at peace with God and men.

I do not say he was at peace with little boys, because our Ignacio was not, strictly speaking, a little boy. He was fifteen, a good, well-grown fifteen. A shaggy untaught head, but handsome, full of questions, a head that wanted to understand and never understood anything, set on a body that was not devoid of grace, though poorly dressed. The father was a barber in Cidade Nova and had placed him as helper, clerk, what-you-will, with the lawyer Borges, in the hope of seeing him practice at the bar because he had noticed that lawyers make lots of money.

The above scene took place on the Rua da Lapa in 1870.

For some minutes nothing was heard but the rattling of knives and forks and noise of chewing. Borges stuffed himself with lettuce and beef, only stopping, occasionally, to punctuate this gustatory eloquence with a dash of wine; soon he fell silent altogether.

Ignacio ate slowly, not daring to lift his eyes from his plate nor turn them to the place where they had been at the moment the terrible Borges lit into him. The truth is, it would now be very dangerous. His eyes never rested on Dona Severina's arms but what he forgot himself and everything else.

The fault was really Dona Severina's in leaving them naked like that all the time. She wore short-sleeved dresses around the house, the sleeves falling scarcely a finger's length below the shoulder; from there down her arms were bare. They really were handsome and plump, like their mistress, who was rather more solid than delicate. And they did not lose their rosy softness for all their exposure to the air. But, it is only fair to explain, she did not wear them thus out of coquetry; it was simply that she had worn out all her long-sleeved dresses. When she stood, Dona Severina was eye-filling; when she walked, she shook with delightful undulations. Ignacio, however, scarcely ever met her except at table, where, aside from her arms, he could not see much of her. She could not be called pretty; but neither was she ugly. Not a single bit of finery. Even the way she combed her hair amounted to little: she smoothed it back, caught it up, twisted it, and anchored it on top of her head with a tortoise-shell comb her mother had given her. At her throat, a dark scarf; in her ears, nothing. All this and the bloom of twenty-seven good substantial years.

They finished eating. When the coffee appeared, Borges took four cigars out of his pocket, compared them, squeezed them between his fingers, chose one, and put the others back. After lighting the cigar, he propped his elbows on the table and talked to Dona Severina of thirty thousand things that held no interest at all for our Ignacio; but while he talked he was not yelling at him, and *he* could muse at pleasure.

Ignacio drew out his coffee as long as he could. Between sips he smoothed the table cloth, picked imaginary particles of skin off his fingers, or let his eyes travel over the pictures on the dining-room wall, which were two: one of St. Peter and one of

St. John, prints brought from church on feast days and fitted with homemade frames. Let him pretend with St. John, whose youthful head gladdens Catholic imaginations, but with the austere Peter! . . . The only excuse for young Ignacio is that he saw neither the one nor the other: his eyes passed over them as over nothing. He saw only Dona Severina's arms—either because he was stealthily looking at them from under his eyelids, or because their image was impressed on his memory.

"Man alive, aren't you ever going to finish?" suddenly bellowed the lawyer.

There was nothing for it. Ignacio drank the last drop, now cold, and withdrew as usual to his bedroom in the back part of the house. As he entered the room, he made a gesture of anger and despair, and then went to one of the two windows that looked on the sea. Five minutes later, the sight of the water close by and the mountains in the distance brought back the vague, restless feeling of confusion that both tortured and comforted him —something the plant must feel when it puts forth its first bud. He felt a desire to leave, and to stay. He had been there five weeks now, and his life was always the same thing: go out with Borges in the morning, haunt the courts, the record offices—running errands, taking documents to the notary, to process servers, to court stenographers, to justices. In the afternoon he came back to the house, had dinner, and retired to his room till suppertime, had supper, and went to bed. Borges did not permit him intimacy with his family, which consisted only of Dona Severina; Ignacio did not see her more than three times a day, at meals. Five weeks of solitude, of distasteful work, far from his mother and his sisters; five weeks of silence, for he only spoke, now and then, to somebody in the street—at home, never a word.

"Just wait! I'll run away from here and never come back."

But he stayed—caught, and held fast, by the arms of Dona Severina. He had never seen such pretty arms, with such a fresh bloom on them. His upbringing kept him from looking straight at them all at once. In the beginning, he even averted his eyes, ashamed and troubled. Little by little he came to look straight at them, seeing they had no other sleeves but his own eyes. Thus he made their acquaintance, looked long at them, began to love them. At the end of three weeks they were, spiritually speaking, his shelter tents. He bore all the drudgery out there in the world of men, all the loneliness of solitude and silence, all the coarse abuse from his employer: his only pay—a glimpse, three times daily, of that superb pair of arms.

On this day, as night came on and Ignacio lay stretched out in his hammock (he had no other bed), Dona Severina, in the living room at the front of the house, went over the episode at dinner point by point, and, for the first time, she suspected something. She as quickly rejected the idea—a child! But there are ideas of the same race as stubborn flies: no matter how we brush them away, they fly back and light in the same place. Child? He was fifteen, and she had noticed that between the young man's nose and mouth there was the beginning of a trace of fuzz. What wonder if he had fallen in love? And wasn't she pretty? This idea was not rejected, but, rather, fondled and kissed. She recalled his actions, his absent-mindedness, his fits of woolgathering, then one thing, then another; they were all signs . . . and she concluded "yes," he had.

"What's the matter with you?" asked the lawyer after several minutes of silence, as he sprawled on the sofa.

"Me? Nothing."

"Nothing? It looks to me as if you're all asleep around here! Just wait! I know of a good medicine to wake up sleepyheads . . ."

And he went on in the same angry tone, shooting off threats right and left, but actually incapable of carrying them out, because he was coarse and rough, but not really mean. Dona Severina interrupted him to say he was mistaken. She was not asleep, but thinking of her godchild's mother, Dona Fortunata. They had not paid her a visit since Christmas. Why not go over there one of these evenings? Borges retorted that he was too tired, that he worked like a slave and was not about to go making social calls and listen to a lot of silly chitchat. Then he lambasted the godchild's mother and the godchild's father and the godchild himself—not yet out of primary school, a great boy of ten! He, Borges, at ten years of age, could read and write and do sums, not very well perhaps but he could do them. Ten years old! A fine end he'd come to:—a lazy bum in a soldier suit! It would take a taste of army life to straighten him out.

Dona Severina tried to calm him by making excuses: the mother's poverty, the father's run of hard luck; and she gave him some timid caresses, half afraid they might irritate him still further.

Night had now come in earnest: she heard the *tlic* of the street lamp as the gas was lit and saw its great reflection flash in the windows of the house opposite. Borges, wearied from the day, for he really was a worker of the first order, began to close his eyes and fall asleep, leaving her alone in the room, in the darkness, alone with herself and the discovery she had made.

Everything seemed to tell the lady it was true. But this truth, once the first shock of amazement was past, brought her a moral complication that she recognized only by its effects, for she could not make out what it was. She no longer understood her own feelings, and could not see her way. She even thought of telling the lawyer everything, and let him order the brat out of the house. But what was everything? Here she pulled up short. Actually there was nothing more than surmise, coincidence, and perhaps illusion. No, no, it was not illusion. She began to piece together vague clues, looks and gestures, the boy's bashfulness, his fits of absent-mindedness; and she rejected the idea of being mistaken. In a few minutes (O sophistical Nature!), reflecting that it would be wrong to accuse him without grounds, she admitted she might have deceived herself—admitted it for the sole purpose of having an excuse to observe him more closely and determine the actual state of affairs.

That very night, from under her eyelids, Dona Severina examined Ignacio's looks and gestures. She did not succeed in finding out anything, because tea time was short and the young man did not take his eyes off his cup. The next day her observation was more successful, and, on the following days, supremely so. She found that the answer was "yes": she was loved and idolized—an adolescent, virgin love, held back by social chains and by a feeling of inferiority that kept him from recognizing himself for what he was. Dona Severina saw at once she had no cause to fear any disrespect, and she concluded that the best thing was to say nothing to the lawyer: she would spare him an unpleasantness, and the poor child another. By now she had convinced herself he was a child, and she proposed to treat him as coolly as she had heretofore, perhaps with greater coolness. That is what she did. Ignacio could sense that her eyes avoided him, or that she spoke roughly to him, almost as roughly as Borges. Other times, it was true, her voice sounded gentle and even sweet, sweet and tender, like the expression of her eyes—though her eyes were generally turned from him and wandered so constantly elsewhere it was only for repose that they came to light upon his head, and that for a brief instant.

"I'll go away," he would say to himself out in the street, as he had the first few days.

He came back to the house, and he did not go away. Dona Severina's arms enclosed a parenthesis in the middle of the long, tedious sentence of the life he led. And this added clause contained a profound, original idea specially invented by God and the angels for him alone. He stayed on, and his life went on as before. Finally, however, he had to leave, never to return. Here is how and why.

For several days, Dona Severina had treated him with kindness. Her voice, it seemed, had lost its rough tone; it was more than gentle, it was full of tenderness and concern. One day she would warn him not to get in a draft, another not to drink cold water after hot coffee, bits of advice, reminders, attentions of a loving woman and a mother—that flung his soul into still greater disquiet and confusion. He grew so bold one day as to laugh at table, something he had never done. And the lawyer did not rebuke him on this occasion, for it was he who was telling a funny story and no one rebukes a person who is applauding one. For the first time, Dona Severina noticed that the boy's mouth, charming in repose, was no less so when he laughed.

The turmoil in Ignacio's heart kept growing. He tried to calm it, and could not; he did not understand himself. He was not at peace anywhere. He would wake up at night, thinking of Dona Severina. In the street, he would take the wrong turn, go to the wrong address—much oftener even than before. And he never saw a woman, near or far, who did not bring her to mind. When he crossed the threshold on coming home from work, he always felt a kind of wild joy, at times overpowering, when he looked up and saw her peering through the wooden grillwork of the gate at the top of the stairs, as if she had run to see who it was.

One Sunday—he never forgot that Sunday—he was alone in his room, at the window, looking toward the sea, which spoke to him in the same obscure tongue as Dona Severina. He amused himself by watching the sea gulls, as they made great circles in

the air or soared above the water, or merely flapped their wings.
The day was fair beyond description. It was not only a Christian
sabbath, it was an immense sabbath of the universe.

Ignacio passed all his Sundays there, in his room, either at the
window or rereading one of the three little books he had brought
home from the city, tales of olden days, bought for a copper or
two under the bridge to the Largo do Paço. It was two o'clock in
the afternoon. He was tired; he had slept badly the night before
after all the running about of the day. He stretched out in his
hammock, took up one of the little books, *Princess Magalona*,
and began to read.

He could never understand why all the heroines of these old
stories had the same face and figure as Dona Severina; but, the
fact of the matter is, they did. At the end of half an hour he let
the book drop and fixed his eyes on the wall, out of which, five
minutes later, he saw the lady of his dreams emerge. The natural
thing would have been to start in astonishment; but he was not
astonished. Although his eyes were tight shut, he saw her tear
herself loose from the wall, smile, and walk toward the hammock.
It was she all right, and those were her very own arms.

And yet, it is certain that Dona Severina could not have come
out of the wall, even if there had been a door in it, or a hole; she
could not have, for the simple reason that she was at that very
moment in the front room, listening to the lawyer's footsteps as
he went down the stairs. When she heard him reach the bottom,
she went to the window, to see him go out the front door, and she
did not leave the window until he disappeared in the distance,
down the Rua das Mangueiras. Then she went back and sat down
on the sofa. She seemed strangely restless, almost crazy. She
got up and went to the sideboard, where she picked up the water
pitcher and set it down in the same place. Then she walked to
the door, stopped, and came back, as it seemed, without design.
She sat down again, for five or ten minutes. Suddenly it occurred
to her that Ignacio had eaten little at breakfast and had seemed
dejected, and she asked herself if he might not be ill, perhaps
very ill.

She left the living room, went straight down the hall to the
boy's bedroom; the door was wide open. Dona Severina stood
still, looked in and saw him asleep in the hammock, one arm
thrown over the side, and the little book fallen on the floor. His

head was slightly turned toward the door so that she could see the closed eyes, the rebellious hair in disorder, and a great smiling look of happiness on his face.

Dona Severina felt her heart pound, and stepped back. She had dreamt of him during the night; perhaps he was dreaming of her. Since early dawn the boy's likeness had been before her eyes like a temptation of the devil. She drew back another step, then returned, stared at him two, three, five or more minutes. Sleep seemed to accentuate Ignacio's adolescence with an expression that was almost feminine—the look of a little boy.

"A child!" she said to herself in that wordless language we all know. And this idea slowed her racing blood and partly cleared away the clouds from her understanding.

"A child!"

She slowly looked her fill—at the head turned toward her, the arm fallen from the hammock. At the same time that she found him childlike, she also found him handsome, much more handsome than when awake, and one of these ideas corrected and modified the other. Suddenly she shivered and drew back in fear: she had heard a noise close by, in the ironing closet. She went to see. A cat had knocked a bowl on the floor. She stole back softly to look in at Ignacio again, and saw that he lay in a deep sleep. He slept like a log, the child! The noise that had so startled her had not even made him change his position. She stood there, and watched him sleep—sleep, perchance dream!

Oh, that we cannot see the dreams of one another! Dona Severina would have seen herself in the young man's imagination, standing beside the hammock, smiling and quite still. She would have seen herself lean down and take his two hands, raise them to her breast and enfold them in her arms—her marvelous arms. Ignacio, busily making love to *them*, still heard the words of his mistress, words that were beautiful, warm, and above all strange —at least they belonged to some language he did not recognize, though he understood it well enough. Two, three, and four times the figure vanished to return again, coming from the sea, or somewhere else, accompanied by sea gulls, or swinging through the hall with all the lusty grace that was hers. Each time, she leaned down and taking his hands again folded them to her breast. Then, finally, she leaned down further and further . . . until her eager mouth left a kiss on his.

Here dream coincided with reality. And the same mouths were
joined in imagination and outside of it. The difference was that
the vision did not leave him, but the real person had no sooner
completed the gesture than she shrank back clear to the door,
vexed and fearful. She passed quickly down the hall, stunned by
what she had done, looking neither right nor left. In the living
room, she strained her ears, went back into the hall to see if she
could hear any sound that would tell her he was awake, and it
was only after some time that her fear began to pass away.
Really, the child slept like a log! Nothing made him open his
eyes, neither crashing pottery nor real, true kisses.

But, if her fear was passing away, her vexation remained and
increased. Dona Severina could not believe she had done this
thing. She seemed to have swathed her desires in the idea that he
was a beloved child who lay there unconscious and blameless;
and, half mother, half lover she had leaned down and kissed
him. Be that as it may, she was confused, disgusted, out of sorts,
annoyed with herself and with him. The fear that he might be
pretending to sleep began to peep forth in her mind, and made
her shudder.

But the truth is, he slept on and on, and only woke up in time
for dinner. He sat down to table in a gay mood. Although he
found Dona Severina taciturn and severe, and the lawyer as
coarse and rude as on other days, neither the rudeness of the
one nor the severity of the other could dissipate the agreeable
vision that was still with him, nor dull the sensation of the kiss.
He did not notice that Dona Severina was wearing a shawl that
covered her arms. He noticed it later, on Monday, and on Tues-
day, and as late as Saturday, which was the day Borges sent word
to his father that he could no longer remain with him. He did
not do it in anger; he treated him comparatively well, and even
said to him when he left, "If you should need me for anything,
look me up."

"Yes, senhor. And Senhora Dona Severina . . ."

"She's there in her room with a bad headache. Come tomorrow or the day after to say goodbye to her."

Ignacio left without understanding at all. He did not understand the dismissal, nor Dona Severina's complete change toward
him, nor the shawl, nor anything. They had been on such good
terms! She had treated him so kindly! How did it happen that

suddenly . . . He thought about it for a long time and finally decided that some indiscreet glance on his part, some thoughtless act, had offended her. It must have been; and this was the reason for the frozen expression, the shawl over her lovely arms . . . No matter! He would take with him the fragrance of the dream.

And down the years, in other love adventures, more real and lasting, he never again found the thrill of that Sunday on the Rua da Lapa, when he was only fifteen. To this day he often exclaims, without knowing he is mistaken, "And it was a dream! Just a dream!"

Translated by HELEN CALDWELL

The Looking Glass

(Rough draft of a new theory of the human soul)

Four or five gentlemen were debating, one night, various questions of a high, transcendental nature—but without any of the opinions expressed having the slightest effect on their minds. The house was high on the Morro de Santa Thereza; the little sitting room, lighted by candles whose brilliance lost itself mysteriously in the moonlight that came from outside. Between the city with its restless turmoil and adventures, and the sky where the stars winked, in a limpid, peaceful atmosphere sat our four or five metaphysical bloodhounds, amicably solving the most thorny problems of the universe.

Why four or five? Actually there were four talking, but in addition there was a fifth individual in the room, who sat silent, thoughtful, half asleep. His contribution to the argument did not go beyond an occasional grunt of approval. He was the same age as his companions—between forty and fifty, a provincial, a capitalist, intelligent, not without education, and, it would seem, of a sly, caustic turn. He never took part in discussions, excusing himself with a paradox. He said discussion was the polite form of the battle instinct that lies deep in man as a bestial heritage. And, he would add, the seraphim and cherubim never entered into controversies, and they were eternal spiritual perfection.

Since he had made this same excuse that very night, one of those present turned on him and challenged him to back up his position with an example—if he could. Jacobina (that was his name) reflected a moment and answered, "All things considered, perhaps what you ask, sir, is only reasonable."

Suddenly then, in the middle of the night, this strange, unsociable character began to hold forth—not for two or three minutes, but for thirty or forty.

The conversation in its meanderings had chanced upon the nature of the soul, a subject that radically divided the four friends. "So many heads, so many opinions." Not only agreement but even discussion became difficult, if not impossible, because of the horde of questions that grew out of the main trunk of the discussion—and partly too, perhaps, because of the inconsistency and incoherence of the arguments. One of the arguers begged Jacobina to give an opinion of some sort, any sort, if only a conjecture.

"Neither conjecture nor opinion," he replied. "Either one could lead to disagreement, and, as you know, I never argue. But, if you will hear me in silence, I can tell you an incident from my own life that will clarify the whole nature of the matter under consideration. In the first place, there is not one soul, but two . . ."

"Two?"

"Two. Every human being is born with two souls: one that looks from the inside out, another that looks from the outside in . . . No, no! Be as astonished as you please, let your mouths drop open, shrug your shoulders, anything . . . but don't try to answer me. If you attempt to argue the point, I finish my cigar and go home to bed. The exterior soul may be a spirit, an invisible aura, a man, many men, an object, an activity. There are cases, for example, in which a simple shirt button is the whole exterior soul of a person—or it may be the polka, ombre, a book, a machine, a pair of shoes, a melody, a drum, and so forth.

"It's plain that the function of this second soul is, like that of the first, to infuse life. The two of them complete the man, who is, metaphysically speaking, an orange. Whoever loses one of the halves, naturally suffers the loss of half his existence. And there have been cases—they are not at all rare—in which the loss of the exterior soul involved the loss of the entire existence. Shylock, for example. The exterior soul of that Jew was his ducats; to lose them was the same as dying. 'I shall never see my gold again,' he says to Tubal, and, 'Thou stick'st a dagger in my heart.' Consider this remark carefully: the loss of the ducats, his exterior soul, was death to him. You must understand, of course, that the exterior soul does not always remain the same . . ."

"No?"

"No. It can change its nature and its condition. I don't mean certain all-consuming souls, like one's native land, with which

Camoens declared he would die, or worldly power, which was the exterior soul of Caesar and Cromwell. These are energetic and possessive souls; but there are others which, though full of energy, are of a changeable, inconstant nature. There are gentlemen, for example, whose exterior soul in their earliest years is a rattle or a hobby-horse, and later, let's say, the honorary chairmanship of a charity. For my own part, I know a lady—really a lovely girl—who changes her exterior soul five, six times a year. During the season, it's opera. When the season is over, this exterior soul is exchanged for some other—a concert, a ball at the Casino, the Rua do Ouvidor, Petropolis . . ."

"Excuse me, but, this lady . . . who is she?"

"This lady is a relative of the devil, and has the same name. Her name is Legion . . . And there are many similar instances. I myself have experienced such changes of soul. I won't attempt to describe them here; it would take too long. I'll confine myself to the one episode I mentioned. It took place in my twenty-fifth year . . ."

His four companions, eager to hear the promised story, forgot their argument. Blessed curiosity! Thou art not only the soul of civilization, thou art also the apple of concord, a divine fruit and with a far different flavor from that well-known mythological apple! The room, just now noisy with physics and metaphysics, became deathly still. All eyes were on Jacobina, who flicked the ashes from his cigar as he assembled his memories. Then he began.

"I was twenty-five at the time, I was poor, and had just been made a second lieutenant in the national guard. You can't imagine what an event this was at our house. My mother was so proud! So happy! She kept calling me her lieutenant. Cousins, uncles, aunts . . . it was all pure, unmixed joy. In the village, it is true, there were some disgruntled persons, and weeping and wailing and gnashing of teeth, as in the Scriptures. The reason was not hard to find: there were many candidates for the post, and these fellows had lost out. I suppose, too, that part of the dismay was entirely gratuitous, occasioned by nothing more than the distinction itself. I remember that, for a time, certain young men of my acquaintance would give me a fishy eye as they passed me in the street. On the other hand there were many who were pleased with the appointment, and the proof is that a complete military uniform was presented to me by friends . . .

"Well then, it so happened, one of my aunts, Dona Marcolina, the widow of Captain Peçanha, who lived many miles from our village in a remote and lonely section of the country, wanted to see me and begged me to come to her place and bring my uniform. I went, attended by one slave, who returned to the village a few days later because hardly had Aunt Marcolina got me at her house than she wrote my mother she would not let me go for a month at least. How she hugged me! She, too, kept calling me her lieutenant. She pronounced me a handsome devil (she was a jolly woman, my aunt) and declared she envied the girl who would become my wife. She swore there was not a man in the whole province who could hold a candle to me. And it was always 'lieutenant': lieutenant here, lieutenant there, lieutenant every second. I begged her to call me Joãozinho, as she used to. She shook her head, exclaiming, 'No,' that I was 'Senhor Lieutenant.'

"Her brother-in-law, the late Peçanha's brother, who lived on the place, never addressed me in any other way either. It was 'Senhor Lieutenant,' not in fun but seriously, and in front of the slaves, who naturally did the same. At table I was given the place of honor and was the first to be served. You can't imagine! If I were to tell you that Aunt Marcolina's enthusiasm rose to such a pitch that she had an enormous mirror placed in my bedroom! It was a rich, magnificent piece that stood out grotesquely from the rest of the house's furnishings, which were plain and modest . . . It was a mirror her godmother had given her, and *she* had inherited it from her mother, who had bought it from one of the Portuguese noblewomen that came in the retinue of Dom João VI in 1808. I don't know how much truth there was in all this: it was family tradition. Anyway, the mirror was very old; but you could still see the gold, partly eaten away by time, some dolphins carved in the upper corners of the molding, mother-of-pearl trimming, and other artistic flourishes. All old, but good . . ."

"An enormous mirror?"

"Enormous. It was, really, awfully kind of my aunt, because the mirror had been in the parlor, and was the finest piece of furniture in the house. But she could not be budged from her purpose. She said no one would miss it, that it was only for a few weeks, and, after all, 'Senhor Lieutenant' deserved much more.

"What is absolutely certain is that all these things—the petting, the attentions, the deference—produced a transformation in me, which the natural feelings of youth added to and completed. You know what I mean, don't you?"

"No."

"The lieutenant eliminated the man. For several days the two natures see-sawed back and forth, but it was not long before the aboriginal me gave way to the other, and I was left with only a trifling part of my well-rounded humanity. What happened was, the exterior soul, which before that time had been the sun, the air, the countryside, and young ladies' eyes, changed in nature and came to be the bowing and scraping at the farmhouse— everything that reminded me of the officer, nothing, of the man. The only part of the citizen that was left me was the part that related to the exercise of military privilege; the other part had melted into the air and the past. You can hardly believe it, eh?"

"I can hardly understand it," retorted one of his hearers.

"You will. My actions will explain my sensations. Actions are everything. The best definition of love in the world is not worth one kiss from the girl you love, and, if I remember rightly, an ancient philosopher proved the reality of motion by walking. Let us get to the actions. Let us see how at the very time the consciousness of the man was being blotted out of existence that of the lieutenant came intensely alive. Human ills, human joys, if it came to that, got scarcely more from me than apathetic pity or a condescending smile. At the end of three weeks I was a different entity, completely different. I was exclusively second lieutenant.

"Then, one day, Aunt Marcolina received bad news: a daughter, married to a landowner and living twenty miles from there, was ill and at death's door. Nephew be hanged! Lieutenant be hanged! She was a doting mother. She packed her bag, asked her brother-in-law to accompany her, and me to take charge of the farm. I believe that, if she had not been so upset, she would have arranged it the other way round: she would have left her brother-in-law in charge and taken me with her.

"However that may be, I stayed behind, alone except for the slaves. At once I had a suffocating sense of oppression, as if four prison walls had suddenly closed round me. Actually, it was my exterior soul, which had begun to shrink. It was now reduced to a handful of ignorant and uncouth minds who could scarcely speak the language. The *lieutenant* continued to dominate in me, but its life-force was less intense, its conscious existence weak. The slaves put a note of humility in their attentions, which, after a fashion, made up for the petting of relatives and the family intimacy that had suddenly been broken off. Even that night, I noticed, they redoubled their respectfulness, their cheerfulness, their protestations. It was 'Nho* Lieutenant' every second: 'Nho Lieutenant very handsome,' 'Nho Lieutenant soon be colonel,' 'Nho Lieutenant marry pretty girl, general's daughter . . .' a chorus of praise and happy auguries that left me ecstatic. Ah! the traitors! How was I to suspect their secret intention?"

"To kill you?"

"If it had been only that!"

"Something worse?"

"Listen. The next morning I found that I was alone. The rascals, led on by others, or in a spontaneous spirit of revolt, had plotted to run away during the night; and that's what they did. I was alone, no one but me, alone between four walls. The terrace was deserted, the fields abandoned. Not a breath of human life anywhere. I ran through the whole house, the slaves' quarters, everywhere. Nothing, no one, not a single pickaninny left behind. Cocks and hens, that was all, a pair of mules philosophizing about life and shaking off flies, and three oxen. Even the dogs had been carried off by the slaves. Not one human being! You think this was better than being killed? It was worse.

"Not that I was afraid, I swear I was not afraid. I was even rather brave . . . I didn't mind the first few hours. I was sorry about the loss to Aunt Marcolina, and uncertain whether I ought to go to her and give her the sorrowful news, or stay and keep watch over the farm. I adopted the second course, in order not to leave the place unprotected; and, if my cousin was seriously ill I would only be adding to the mother's distress to no purpose. Besides, I hoped Uncle Peçanha's brother would return that day or the next, seeing he had already been gone thirty-six hours. But the morning passed without any trace of him. In the afternoon

* Corruption of *senhor.*

I began to have a feeling that my nerves no longer functioned, and that I had lost control over my muscles.

"Uncle Peçanha's brother did not return that day nor the next, nor all that week. My solitude took on enormous proportions. Never had days been so long, never had the sun burned into the earth with such tiresome obstinacy. The hours were sounded from century to century by the old clock in the parlor, and the tick-tock, ticktock of its pendulum flicked my inner soul like a constant fillip of eternity. Many years later, when I read an American poem—I think it was one of Longfellow's—and came across the famous refrain *Never, for ever! For ever, never!,* I tell you, it made me shiver, and I thought back to those dreadful days. It was just so with Aunt Marcolina's clock, *Never, for ever! For ever, never!* They were not strokes of a pendulum: they were a dialogue from the pit, a whisper from the void. And then at night! Not that the night was more silent. Its silence was the same as the day's. But the night was shadow, it was solitude still more close than the solitude of day, or more vast. Ticktock, ticktock. No one in the great rooms, nor on the veranda, no one in the halls, no one on the terrace, no one anywhere . . . you're laughing?"

"Yes, I'd say you were just a little bit afraid."

"Oh! It would have been good if I could have felt fear! I would have been alive. But the odd thing was I could not feel fear—fear, that is, in the ordinary sense of the word. I was held by an unaccountable sensation—as if I was a walking dead man, a somnambulist, a mechanical toy. Sleep, real sleep, was another matter: it brought me relief—not for the usual reason, that it is the brother of death—but, for another. I believe I can best explain it in this way. Sleep, eliminating the necessity for an exterior soul, permitted the inner soul to go into action. At night, in my dreams, I wore my uniform, proudly, in the midst of family and friends, who praised my gallant bearing and called me lieutenant. And there came a family friend and promised me the rank of first lieutenant, another the rank of captain or of major. All this breathed life into me. But when I awoke in the bright light of broad day, the conscious life of my new one-souled being evaporated with the dream, because my inner soul had lost its exclusive power of action and was now dependent on the other, the exterior soul, which stubbornly persisted in not coming back. "And it continued to not come back. I would go outside, look this way and that, to see if I could discover some token of return. 'Soeur Anne, soeur Anne, ne vois-tu rien venir?' Nothing, not a thing—just as in the French fairy tale. Only the dust on the road and the grass growing on the hill. I would go back into the house, nervous and depressed, and stretch out on the sofa in the parlor. Ticktock, ticktock. I'd get up, walk about, beat a tattoo on the window pane, whistle. At one point I decided to write something . . . a political article, a novel, an ode: I didn't go so far as to make a definite choice. I sat down and scrawled some disconnected words and sentences on the paper, to work up my style. But the style, like Aunt Marcolina, would not come. *Soeur Anne, soeur Anne* . . . Nothing at all. At most, I saw the ink blacken and the paper grow white."

"Didn't you eat?"

"Very little, fruits, manioc meal, canned stuff, some roots roasted in the fire, but I would gladly have endured everything if it had not been for the dreadful mental state I was in. I recited over verses, speeches, fragments of Latin, love poems by Gonzaga, stanzas of Camoens, snatches of sonnets—an anthology in thirty volumes. Sometimes I did gymnastic exercises, at other times I pinched my legs; but the result was only a physical sensation of pain, or of weariness, nothing more. Everywhere: a vast, measureless, infinite silence underscored by the eternal ticktock of the old pendulum clock. Ticktock, ticktock . . ."

"Enough to drive a man crazy."

"But you haven't heard the worst. I should tell you that since I had been alone, I had not once glanced into the mirror. I didn't avoid it deliberately; I had no reason for doing so. It was an unconscious impulse, a dread of discovering that there in that solitary house I was both one and two. If this explanation is the true one, there is no better proof of human contradiction, because at the end of a week I took it into my head to look into the mirror for the precise purpose of finding myself two. I looked, and I drew back. The glass itself, along with the rest of the universe, seemed to have conspired against me. It did not stamp out my image sharp and complete, but vague, misty, diffuse, a shadow of a shadow. The reality of the laws of physics does not permit me to deny that the mirror faithfully reproduced me with my very own shape and features. It must have. But that was not what I saw.

"I was frightened. I laid the thing to my 'nerves.' I was afraid if I stayed longer I'd go crazy. 'I'll leave,' I said to myself. And I raised my arm in an ill-humored gesture. At the same time, it was a gesture of determination. I glanced at the mirror: the gesture was there, but shattered, frayed, mutilated . . . I began to get dressed, muttering to myself as I did so, clearing my throat, noisily shaking out my garments, and coldly communicating my grievance to my buttons just to be saying something. From time to time I glanced furtively toward the mirror: the image was the same dispersal of streaks, the same watery outlines . . . I went on dressing. Suddenly, by some unaccountable inspiration, a sudden impulse, the idea occurred to me . . . You'll never guess what it was . . ."

"What? What was it?"

"I was looking into the mirror with the persistence of desperation, contemplating my own disconnected and incomplete features, a mist of loose, misshapen lines, when I got the idea . . . No, you could never guess what it was."

"Go on, tell us! What was it?"

"I got the idea of putting on my lieutenant's uniform. I put it on, the whole outfit. As I was standing in front of the mirror, I raised my eyes, and . . . (no doubt you've guessed) the glass now reproduced the complete figure, not a line missing, not a feature awry. It was me, the second lieutenant, who had finally found his exterior soul. This soul that had gone off with the mistress of the place, that had scattered and fled with the slaves, there it was, put together again in the looking glass. Imagine a man who little by little emerges from a coma, opens his eyes without seeing, then begins to see, distinguishes people from things but does not yet recognize them as individuals, then finally knows that this is Peter, that is Paul, here is a chair, there a sofa. Everything returns to what it was before he sank into the sleep. So it was with me. I stared into the mirror, moved from side to side, backed away, gesticulated, smiled, and the glass revealed everything. I was no longer an automaton; I was an animated, living thing.

"From then on I was another man. Each day, at a certain

time, I would dress up in my lieutenant's outfit and sit down before the mirror, while I read, looked, and meditated. At the end of two or three hours I would take it off again. By strictly adhering to this regimen, I was able to live through six more days of solitude without feeling them . . ."

When the others in the room came to, the storyteller had reached the bottom of the stairs on his way to the street.

Translated by HELEN CALDWELL

The Secret Heart

Garcia, who was standing, studied his finger nails, and snapped them from time to time. Fortunato, in the rocking chair, looked at the ceiling. Maria Luiza, by the window, was putting the final touches to a piece of needlework. Five minutes had now passed without their saying a word. They had spoken of the day, which had been fine, of Catumby, where Fortunato and his wife lived, and of a private hospital that will be explained later.

They had also spoken of something else, something so grim and unpleasant that it took away all desire to talk of the day, the surroundings, and the hospital. Their conversation in respect to it had been constrained. Even now, Maria Luiza's hands still trembled, while Garcia's face had a severe look—something not usual with him. As a matter of fact, what happened was of such a nature that to make the situation clear it will be necessary to go back to its very beginning.

Garcia had obtained his M.D. the year before, 1861. In the year 1860, while he was still in medical school, he had seen Fortunato for the first time, at the entrance to the Santa Casa hospital. He was going in as the other was coming out. He had been struck by Fortunato's appearance, but even so would have forgotten him, if it had not been for a second encounter only a few days later. He lived on the Rua Dom Manuel. One of his rare diversions was to go to the Theater São Januário, which was close by, between that street and the bay. He was in the habit of going once or twice a month, and never found more than forty persons in the audience. Only the most intrepid were bold enough to extend their travels to that out-of-the-way corner of the city. One night as he was sitting in the orchestra, Fortunato came in and sat down beside him.

The play was a heavy melodrama, stabbed through and through with daggers, bristling with curses and remorse, but Fortunato heard it with singular interest. In the painful scenes his attention redoubled, his eyes kept going avidly from one character to another—so much so that the medical student began to suspect that the play stirred personal memories in the man. At the end of the drama, a farce came on, but Fortunato did not wait to see it, and left the theater. Garcia followed him. Fortunato went down the Beco do Cotovelo, along the Rua de São José to the Largo da Carioca. He walked slowly, with lowered head, stopping now and then to whack with his cane some dog that was lying asleep. The dog would howl and *he* would keep on going. In the Largo da Carioca he climbed into a Tilbury and went off in the direction of the Praça da Constituição. Garcia went home without learning more than this.

Several weeks passed. One night, about nine o'clock, as he sat at home in his garret apartment, he heard the sound of voices on the stairway. He went down at once to the second floor, where an employee of the Army Arsenal lived: several men were helping him upstairs, and he was covered with blood. His colored serving man came running to the door, the man groaned, there was a jumble of voices, the light was dim. When the wounded man had been set down on his bed, Garcia said they must send for a doctor.

"One's already on the way," someone replied.

Garcia glanced toward the speaker; it was the man he had seen at the hospital and in the theater. He supposed he was a relative or friend of the wounded man, but he dismissed the idea when he heard him ask if the fellow had a family or any close relative. The colored man said he had not; then the stranger took full charge. He asked the others to leave, paid the porters, and gave the necessary orders for seeing to the wounded man. Learning that Garcia was a neighbor and a medical student, he asked him to remain and assist the doctor. Then he told what had happened.

"It was a gang of *capoeiras*.* I was coming from the Moura Barracks, where I had gone to visit a cousin, when I heard a lot

* Members of gangs who menaced the streets of Rio de Janeiro during the greater part of the nineteenth century. They were finally wiped out by Ferraz, the first police chief of the Republic, in 1890.

of yelling and then a scuffle. It seems they wounded another fellow who was going by and he turned down one of those side streets, but all I saw was this gentleman, who was crossing the street, at the moment one of the ruffians brushed against him and stuck a dagger in him. He didn't fall immediately; he told me where he lived, and, since it was but a few steps away, I thought it best to bring him home."

"Did you know him before?" asked Garcia.

"No, I'd never laid eyes on him. Who is he?"

"He's a good man, an employee of the Army Arsenal. His name is Gouvêa."

"No, I don't know him."

The doctor and the police inspector soon arrived. The man's wound was dressed, and the information taken down. The stranger said his name was Fortunato Gomes da Silveira, that he was a bachelor, living on his income, a resident of Catumby. The wound was considered serious. While it was being dressed with the help of the medical student, Fortunato acted as servant, holding the basin, the candle, the cloths, without fuss, and looking coldly at the wounded man, who groaned a good deal. Afterwards he had a private conversation with the doctor, walked with him as far as the landing, and again assured the inspector that he was ready to assist the police with their investigation. After these two had left, he and the medical student remained in the bedroom. Garcia was dumbfounded. He glanced toward him, saw him calmly sit down, stretch out his legs, put his hands in his trousers pockets, and fix his eyes on the sick man. His eyes were a clear gray, the color of lead, they moved slowly and had a hard, cold, indifferent expression. His face was thin and pale, with a narrow band of sparse red beard clipped close and extending from beneath his chin to either temple. He was perhaps forty years old. From time to time he turned to the student and asked some question about the wounded man, but immediately returned his gaze to him while the young man answered. The feeling the student got was at once one of repulsion and of curiosity; he could not deny that he was witnessing an act of rare dedication, and, if he was disinterested, as he seemed, there was nothing else to do but accept the human heart as a well of mysteries.

It was almost one o'clock when Fortunato left. He returned

on the succeeding days, but the cure progressed rapidly, and before it was completed he disappeared without telling the wounded man where he lived. It was the student who gave him the information as to name, street, and number.

"I'm going to thank him for the kindness he did me, as soon as I can go out," said the convalescent.

Six days afterward, he hurried to Catumby. Fortunato received him with a constrained air, listened impatiently to his words of thanks, replied in a bored manner, and ended by swinging the cord of his dressing gown against his knee. Gouvêa, sitting silent before him, smoothed his hat with his fingers, lifted his eyes from time to time without finding anything to say. At the end of ten minutes he asked permission to leave, and left.

"Watch out for *capoeiras!*" said his host with a laugh.

The poor devil left there mortified, humiliated, scarcely able to swallow his dislike, making an effort to forget it, to explain it away or excuse it, so that only the memory of the kind deed would remain in his heart, but the effort was vain. Resentment, a new and exclusive lodger moved in and kicked out the kind deed so that the poor thing had no recourse but to climb up into the brain and take refuge there as a mere idea. So it was that the benefactor himself forced upon this man the sentiment of ingratitude.

All this astonished Garcia. The young man possessed in germ the ability to decipher men, to unravel human character. He had a love of analysis, and felt a special pleasure, which he called exquisite, in penetrating layer after layer of spiritual strata until he touched the secret heart of an organism. Pricked on by curiosity, he thought of going to see the man of Catumby, but it occurred to him that he had not received a definite invitation to call on him. He needed an excuse, at least, and he could think of none.

Many months later, after he had obtained his degree and was living on the Rua de Matacavallos, near the Rua do Conde, he happened to meet Fortunato on an omnibus, and he ran into him a number of other times: these meetings brought acquaintance. One day Fortunato invited him to come visit him in near-by Catumby.

"Did you know I was married?"

"No."

"I got married four months ago—it seems like four days. Come have dinner with us Sunday."

"Sunday?"

"Don't go making up excuses. I won't take excuses. Come, Sunday."

Garcia went on Sunday. Fortunato gave him a good dinner, good cigars, and good conversation, in company with his wife, who was interesting. He had not changed in appearance. His eyes were the same steely disks, hard and cold; his other features were no more attractive than before. His courtesy, however, if it did not redeem his nature, at least offered considerable compensation. It was Maria Luiza who possessed charm both of person and of manners. She was slender and graceful, with gentle, submissive eyes. She was twenty-one, and looked nineteen. The second time Garcia went there he noticed a certain dissonance in their natures, that little or no spiritual affinity existed between them, and in the wife's manner toward her husband there was something that went beyond respect and bordered on subjection and fear. One day when the three were together, Garcia asked Maria Luiza if she knew the circumstances under which he had met her husband.

"No," she answered.

"You are going to hear of a handsome deed."

"It's not worth the telling," interrupted Fortunato.

"She shall decide whether it's worth telling or no," insisted the doctor.

He told the story of the Rua Dom Manuel. The girl listened in amazement. Little by little she stretched out her hand and clasped her husband's wrist; she was smiling and grateful, as if she had just discovered his heart. Fortunato shrugged his shoulders but he did not hear the tale with indifference. At the end of it, he himself told of the visit the wounded man had paid him, with all the details of his appearance, gestures, his hesitant words, tongue-tied silences—in short a clown. And he kept laughing as he told it. It was not the laughter of a two-faced man, which is evasive and sly. *His* laugh was frank and genial.

"A strange fellow!" thought Garcia.

Maria Luiza was upset by her husband's mockery, but Garcia restored her to her former contentment by again mentioning his dedication and rare qualities as a nurse—"such a good nurse," he concluded, "that if I ever start a private hospital, I'll ask him to be my partner."

"You mean it?"

"Mean what?"

"That we are going to start a hospital?"

"No, I was joking."

"We *could* do it. And for you, just beginning your practice, it might not be a bad idea. It so happens I have a house that is going to fall vacant; it will be the very thing."

Garcia refused to consider the proposal on that day, and on the next; but the idea had become fixed in the other's head, and he would not be put off. As a matter of fact, it would be a good beginning for a doctor, and might turn out to be a good business for both of them. Garcia definitely accepted a few days later. It was a disappointment to Maria Luiza. The high-strung, delicate girl suffered at the very thought of her husband living in contact with human illnesses, but she did not dare oppose him, and bowed her head. The plans were quickly drawn up and carried into effect. The truth is, Fortunato gave no thought to anything else, either then or later. After the hospital opened, it was he who served as administrator and head nurse: he inspected everything, supervised everything—purchases, broths, drugs, and accounts.

Garcia could see that the dedication to the wounded man on the Rua Dom Manuel was not a matter of chance but suited with his nature. He saw him perform menial and obnoxious tasks: he did not shrink from anything, did not find any disease distressing or repulsive, and was ready for anything at any time of day or night. Everyone admired and applauded. Fortunato studied, and closely followed the operations. He, and he alone, handled the caustics. "I have great faith in caustics," he would say.

The sharing of a common interest tightened the bonds of friendship. Garcia became a familiar of the house. He dined there almost every day, and there he observed Maria Luiza and saw her life of spiritual loneliness. And somehow this loneliness of hers increased her loveliness. Garcia began to feel troubled when she came into the room, when she spoke, when she worked quietly by the window, or played sweet, sad music on the piano. Gently, imperceptibly, love entered his heart. When he found it there, he tried to thrust it out, that there might be no other bond but friendship between him and Fortunato. But he did not

succeed. He succeeded only in locking it in. Maria Luiza understood—both his love and his silence—but she never let on.

In the beginning of October, something happened that opened
the doctor's eyes still more to the young woman's plight. Fortunato had taken up the study of anatomy and physiology, and
busied himself in his spare time with ripping open and poisoning
cats and dogs. Since the animals' cries disturbed the patients,
he moved his laboratory home, and his wife, with her nervous
temperament, had to endure them. One day, when she could
stand no more, she went to the doctor and asked him to get her
husband—as if it was his own idea—to give up these experiments.

"But you yourself . . ."

Maria Luiza answered with a smile. "He probably considers
me childish. What I would like is for you, as a doctor, to tell him
that this is bad for me. And, believe me, it is."

Garcia promptly got Fortunato to put an end to these experiments. If he performed them somewhere else, no one knew
of it, but it may be that he did. Maria Luiza thanked the physician not only for herself but also for the animals, which she could
not see suffer. She coughed, as she spoke. Garcia asked her if
she was ill. She answered, "No."

"Let me feel your pulse."

"There's nothing wrong with me."

She did not let him feel her pulse, and went out of the room.
Garcia was worried. He thought, on the contrary, there might be
something wrong with her, that it was necessary to observe her
and warn her husband in time.

Two days later—it was the very day on which we first
glimpsed them—Garcia came to dinner. In the hall he was told
that Fortunato was in his study, and he started toward that
room. As he arrived at the study door, Maria Luiza came out in
a state of great distress.

"What's the matter?" he asked.

"The rat! the rat!" she cried in a choked voice and went on.

Garcia remembered hearing Fortunato complain the day
before of a rat that had carried off an important paper, but he
never expected to see what he did see. He saw Fortunato seated
at the table, which was in the middle of the study, and on which
was placed a plate with spirits of alcohol in it. The liquid was on
fire. Between the thumb and index finger of his left hand For-

tunato held a hook from the point of which the rat hung by its tail. In his right hand he had a pair of scissors. At the moment Garcia entered the room, he was cutting off one of the rat's paws. Then he lowered the poor thing into the flame, rapidly in order not to kill it, and made ready to do the same to the third paw, for he had already cut off the first. Garcia stopped short in horror.

"Kill it at once!" he said.

"In a minute."

And with a strange smile, reflection of a soul replete with satisfaction, a smile that told of an inward savoring of the most exquisite sensation, Fortunato cut off the rat's third paw, and for the third time made the same movement into the flame. The wretched animal squealed and twisted its bloodied, singed body, and would not die. Garcia turned away his eyes, then looked again, and put out his hand as if to prevent the torture from continuing, but he did not complete the gesture, because the devil of a man compelled fear, with that radiant serenity of countenance.

It only remained to cut off the fourth paw. He cut it off very slowly, keeping his eyes on the scissors. The paw dropped and he remained looking at the rat, now half cadaver. He lowered it into the flame for the fourth time, still more rapidly, to save if he could some tatters of life.

Garcia, who stood on the other side of the table, mastered his repugnance and looked intently at Fortunato's face. Neither rage nor hate; only a vast pleasure, quiet and deep, such pleasure as another man might derive from hearing a beautiful sonata or from seeing a sublime statue—something resembling pure, aesthetic feeling. It appeared to Garcia, and it was actually the case, that Fortunato had entirely forgotten him. He could not have been putting it on, no, it was impossible. The flame was dying, it may have been that the rat still had a bit of life left, a shadow of a shadow: Fortunato took advantage of it to cut off the animal's little muzzle, and, for the last time, to bring its flesh to the flame. Finally he let the dead thing drop on the plate, and pushed from him all that mess of scorched flesh and blood.

As he stood up he came face to face with the physician and started. *Then* he displayed rage against the animal that had carried off his paper, but the anger was plainly counterfeit.

"Punishment without anger," thought the doctor, "the need

for a sensation of pleasure that only another creature's pain can give—that is the secret heart of this man."

Fortunato expatiated upon the importance of the document . . . only loss of time, it was true, but time was precious to him right now. Garcia listened without a word, without belief. He recalled other actions of Fortunato's, serious and trifling things: he found the same explanation for all of them, a ringing of changes on the same set of sensations, a unique kind of dilettantism—a miniature Caligula.

When Maria Luiza returned to the study a few minutes later, her husband went up to her, laughingly took her hands, and said gently, "Coward!" And, turning toward the doctor, "Would you believe it? She almost fainted."

Maria Luiza timidly protested: she was nervous, and a woman. Then she went and sat by the window, with her colored wools and needles, and her fingers still trembling, just as we saw her at the beginning of this story. It will be recalled that after speaking of other matters, the three fell silent: the husband sat looking at the ceiling, the physician snapping his finger nails.

Not long after, they went in to dinner; but dinner was not cheerful. Maria Luiza's thoughts kept straying and she coughed frequently. The doctor asked himself if she might not be exposed to some vicious excess in the company of such a man. It was barely possible, but his love transformed the possibility into a certainty: he trembled for her and determined to keep a close watch over both of them.

Her cough grew worse, and it was not long before the disease put off its mask. It was tuberculosis, insatiate old hag that sucks the life and leaves a pulp of bones. Fortunato received the news as a blow. He really loved his wife, in his way, was used to her, it was hard to lose her. He spared nothing—doctors, medicines, change of air, all the remedies, all the palliatives. But it was in vain. The illness was mortal.

In the final days, in the presence of her last terrible torments, the husband's peculiar bent dominated whatever other feeling he may have had. He never left her for an instant, fastened a cold, dull eye on that slow, painful dissolution of life, drank in, one by one, the suffering moments of this beautiful woman, now thin and transparent, consumed by fever and sapped by death. His relentless egoism, ravening after sensations, refused to renounce a single minute of her agony, or repay her with a single tear, in public or in private. Only when she died—then he was stunned. When he came to his senses he saw that he was again alone.

In the night, a female relative of Maria Luiza's, who had been with her when she died, went to get some rest. Fortunato and Garcia stayed on in the parlor, watching with the corpse, both thoughtful. But the husband, too, was exhausted. The doctor told him to rest for a while.

"Go lie down and sleep for an hour or two. I'll do the same afterward."

Fortunato went into an adjoining sitting room, stretched out on the sofa, and fell asleep at once. Twenty minutes later he awoke, tried to go back to sleep, dozed a few minutes, then got up and returned to the parlor. He walked on tiptoe so as not to awaken the relative, who was asleep close by. As he reached the door, he stopped in astonishment.

Garcia had gone up to the corpse, had raised the face-covering and gazed for some seconds at the dead woman's features. Then, as if death spiritualized everything, he leaned down and kissed her forehead. It was at this moment that Fortunato reached the door. He stopped in astonishment. Impossible that it was the kiss of friendship, it must have been the epilogue to a long book of adultery. He was not jealous, be it noted. Nature had so mixed the elements in him as not to give him either jealousy or envy, but she had given him vanity, which is no less subject to resentment. He stared in astonishment, biting his lips.

Meanwhile, Garcia again leaned down to kiss the dead woman; but this time he could not bear his grief. The kiss gave way to sobs, and his eyes could no longer hold their tears, which poured forth in a flood, tears of love that had been stilled—of love and of hopeless despair. Fortunato, from the doorway, where he had remained, quietly savored this outburst of spiritual pain, which was long, very long, delightfully long.

Translated by HELEN CALDWELL

The Rod of Justice

Damião ran away from the seminary at eleven o'clock in the morning, on a Friday in August. I am not sure of the year, but it was before 1850.* After a few minutes he stopped in embarrassment. He had not counted on the effect his appearance would have on other people—a seminarist in his cassock, hurrying along with a dazed, fearful look. He did not recognize the streets, he kept missing his way and retracing his steps. Finally he stopped altogether. Where would he go? Home? No, that was where his father was, and his father would send him back to the seminary, after a good trouncing. He had not settled upon a place of refuge, because his departure had been planned for a later date: an unforeseen circumstance hastened it. Where would he go? He thought of his godfather, João Carneiro, a soft muttonhead with no will of his own. He'd be of no help. It was he who took him to the seminary in the first place and presented him to the rector.

"I bring you the great-man-to-be," he had said to the rector.

"Let him enter, let the great man enter, provided he be also meek and good. True greatness is humble. Young man . . ."

Such was his introduction. Not long after, he ran away. And now we see him in the street, dazed, uncertain, with no idea of where to take refuge, or even ask for advice. He mentally ran over the houses of relatives and friends without regarding any one of them with much favor. Suddenly he cried out, "I'll go beg Sinhá† Rita to protect me! She will send for my godfather, tell him that she wants me to leave the seminary . . . Maybe . . ."

Sinhá Rita was a widow, the sweetheart of João Carneiro. Damião had certain vague ideas about this situation and decided

* Date of suppression of the slave trade.
† Appellation used by slaves for *senhora,* "mistress."

76

to turn it to his advantage. Where did she live? He was so confused that it was several minutes before he could remember
where her house was. It was in the Largo do Capim.

"Holy name of Jesus! What's this?" screamed Sinhá Rita sitting upright on the settee where she had been reclining. Damião
entered terror-stricken. At the very moment of reaching the house,
he had seen a priest walking along, had given the door a shove,
and by great good luck it was neither locked nor bolted. Once
inside, he peeked through the lattice to watch the padre. The
latter had not noticed him, and kept on his way.

"But what's this, Senhor Damião?" the mistress of the house
again screamed, for it was only now that she recognized him.
"What are you doing here?"

Damião, trembling, scarcely able to speak, told her not to be
afraid, it was nothing, he would explain everything.

"There, there, go ahead and explain."

"First of all, I have not perpetrated any crime, that I swear!
Wait."

Sinhá Rita looked at him with a startled air, and all the little
slave girls—those of the household and those from outside—who
were seated around the room before their work cushions, all
stopped moving their bobbins and their hands. Sinhá Rita made
her living, for the most part, by teaching lacemaking, drawn work,
and embroidery. While the boy caught his breath, she ordered
the little girls back to work, and waited. At last Damião poured
out everything: the misery the seminary caused him, he was sure
he could never be a good padre. He spoke with passion and
begged her to save him.

"How? I can't do anything."

"Yes, you can, if you really want to."

"No," she answered, shaking her head, "I'm not butting into
your family's affairs. I scarcely know them. And your father—
they say he has a terrible temper!"

Damião saw his hopes fading. He knelt at her feet, kissed
her hands in desperation.

"You can do a great deal, Sinhá Rita. I beg you for the love
of God—by whatever you hold most sacred, by the soul of your
late husband—save me from death, because I'll kill myself if I
have to go back to that place."

Sinhá Rita, flattered by the young man's entreaties, tried to recall him to a more cheerful frame of mind. A priest's life was holy and fine, she told him, time would teach him it was better to overcome one's dislikes, and one day . . .

"No, nohow, never!" he retorted shaking his head and kissing her hands, and he kept repeating that it would be his death.

Even then, Sinhá Rita hesitated, for a long time. Finally she asked him why he did not go talk to his godfather.

"My godfather? He's even worse than papa, he doesn't pay any attention to what I say, I don't believe he'd pay attention to anyone . . ."

"No?" interrupted Sinhá Rita, her pride pricked. "Well, I'll show him whether he'll pay attention or not . . ."

She called a slave and ordered him in a loud voice to go to João Carneiro's house and tell him to come at once, and if he was not at home to ask where he could be found, and to run and tell him that she had to speak to him immediately.

"Get along, darky!"

Damião sighed heavily.

To cover up the authority with which she had given these orders, she explained to the youth that Senhor João Carneiro had been a friend of her dead husband and had got her some of these slaves as pupils. Then, as Damião continued to lean gloomily against the door jamb, she smiled and tweaked his nose, "Come, come, your reverence! Don't worry, everything will be all right."

Sinhá Rita was forty years old by her baptismal certificate, but her eyes were seven and twenty. She was a fine figure of a woman, lively, merry, and fond of a joke, but, if need be, fierce as the devil. She set out to cheer the boy up, and it was not hard for her. In a little while they were both laughing: she told him funny stories and asked him to tell her some, which he did with singular wit and charm. One of them, thanks to his crazy capering and grimacing, was so absurd that it made one of Sinhá Rita's pupils laugh: she had forgotten her work to stare at the young man and listen to him. Sinhá Rita grabbed a birch rod that was lying beside the settee and called out in a threatening voice, "Lucretia, mind the rod!"

The little girl lowered her head to parry the blow, but the blow did not fall. It was a warning. If her task was not finished at nightfall, Lucretia would receive the usual punishment. Damião looked at the child: she was a little Negress, a frail wisp of a thing with a scar on her forehead and a burn on her left hand. She was eleven years old. Damião noticed that she kept coughing, but inwardly, and muffled, so as not to interrupt the conversation. He was sorry for the little black girl, and resolved to protect her if she did not finish her task. Sinhá Rita would not refuse to forgive her . . . Besides, she had laughed because she found him amusing; the fault was his, if it is a fault to be witty.

At this point, João Carneiro arrived. He turned pale when he saw his godson there, and looked at Sinhá Rita, who wasted no time in preliminaries. She told him it was necessary to remove the boy from the seminary, that he had no talent for an ecclesiastical life, and better one priest the less than a bad priest. One could love and serve Our Lord out in the world just as well.

João Carneiro was thunderstruck. For several minutes he could find nothing to say. Finally he opened his mouth and began to reprimand his godson for coming and bothering "strangers," and then he asserted he would punish him.

"Punish, nothing!" interrupted Sinhá Rita. "Punish for what? Go on, go talk to the boy's father."

"I don't guarantee anything. I don't believe it will be possible to . . ."

"And I guarantee it will be possible, it has to be. If you have a will to do it, senhor," she continued in an insinuating tone, "everything is bound to be arranged. Keep after him; he'll give in. Get along, João Carneiro, your godson is not going back to the seminary. I tell you, he is not going back . . ."

"But, my dear senhora . . ."

"Go, go on."

João Carneiro was in no hurry to leave, and he could not remain. He was caught between two opposing forces. It really made no difference to him whether his godson ended up a priest, a doctor, a lawyer, or what—even if he turned out to be a good-for-nothing bum and loafer. But, the worst of it was, he was being pushed into a terrible struggle against the most intimate feelings of his friend the boy's father, with no certainty as to the result. If the result proved negative, he would have another fight on his hands with Sinhá Rita, whose final words were, "I tell you he is not going back." There was bound to be a row. João Carneiro's gaze became unsteady, his eyelids twitched, his chest heaved, and the eyes he turned upon Sinhá Rita were full of supplication, mixed with a mild gleam of censure. Why couldn't she ask something else of him? Why couldn't she command him to walk up Tijuca in a pouring rain, or up Jacarèpaguá? But to persuade his godson's father, like that, to change his son's whole career . . . He knew the man, he was quite capable of breaking a water pitcher over his head. Oh, if his godson would only drop dead, then and there, of a fit of apoplexy! It would be a solution, cruel, it is true, but conclusive.

"Well?" insisted Sinhá Rita.

He held up his hand for her to wait. He scratched his beard, hunting for an expedient. God in heaven! a decree of the pope dissolving the Church, or at the least abolishing seminaries, would fix up everything. João Carneiro would go back home and play *três-setes.* Imagine Napoleon's barber entrusted with the command of the battle of Austerlitz . . . But the Church lived on, seminaries lived on, his godson lived on, shrunk against the wall, his eyes downcast, hoping, and giving no promise of an apoplectic solution.

"Be off, be off," said Sinhá Rita, handing him his hat and cane.

There was no help for it. The barber put the razor in its case, girded on his sword, and sallied forth to battle. Damião began to breathe again. Outwardly, however, he was the same, eyes fixed on the ground, dispirited. This time, Sinhá Rita chucked him under the chin. "Come on to dinner, and stop brooding."

"Do you really think, senhora, that he'll do anything?"

"He'll do everything," she asserted with a self-confident air. "Come along or the soup'll get cold."

In spite of Sinhá Rita's boisterous good humor and his own lighthearted nature, Damião was less cheerful at dinner than he had been earlier in the day. He distrusted his godfather's flabby character. Still, he ate a good dinner, and toward the end returned to his jesting mood of that morning. During dessert he heard the sound of voices in the sitting room and asked if they had come to arrest him.

"It must be the girls."

They got up from the table and went into the other room. The "girls" were five young women of the neighborhood who came every afternoon to take coffee with Sinhá Rita, and stayed until nightfall.

The pupils finished their dinner and returned to their work cushions. Sinhá Rita was mistress of all this womenfolk—slaves of her own household and from outside. The whisper of the bobbins and the chattering of the "girls" were such worldly echoes, so far from theology and Latin, that the young man gave himself up to them and forgot those other things.

During the first few minutes there was a certain constraint on the part of the neighbor women, but it soon wore off. One of them sang a popular song, to a guitar accompaniment played by Sinhá Rita. And so the afternoon passed quickly. Sinhá Rita asked Damião to tell a certain funny story that had particularly delighted her. It was the one that had made Lucretia laugh.

"Come on, Senhor Damião, don't be coy, the girls have to leave. You'll be crazy about it."

There was nothing for Damião to do but obey. Although the announcement and the expectation served to lessen the drollery and the effect, the story ended amid the loud laughter of the girls. Damião, pleased with himself, did not forget Lucretia, and glanced in her direction to see if she had laughed too. He saw her with her head bent over the work cushion, trying to complete her task. She was not laughing, or she may have been laughing inwardly, just as she coughed.

The neighbor women left, and the day was gone in earnest. Damião's soul grew dark before the night. What was happening? Every other second he went and peered through the lattice and returned each time more downhearted. Not a sign of his godfather. It was certain his father had made him shut up, called a couple of slaves, gone to the police station for an officer, and was on his way thither to seize him by force and drag him back to the seminary. He asked Sinhá Rita if the house happened to have a back door, he ran into the yard and figured he could jump over the wall. He tried to find out if there was a way of escape down the Rua da Valla, or if it was better to speak to one of the neighbors, and see if they would take him in. The worst thing was the cassock: if Sinhá Rita could only get him a man's jacket, an old coat . . . Sinhá Rita just happened to have a man's jacket in the house, a remembrance—or a forgetfulness—of João Carneiro.

"I do have a jacket . . . that belonged to my late husband," she said with a laugh, "but why are you so scared? Everything will be all right. Don't worry."

Finally, at nightfall, there appeared one of his godfather's slaves with a letter for Sinhá Rita. The business was not yet settled; the father was furious and wanted to smash things. He had shouted "no sir," the young dandy would go to the seminary, or he would have him locked up in the Aljube or on a prison ship. João Carneiro fought hard to get him not to make a decision right away, to sleep on it, and think over carefully whether it was *right* to offer the Church such an unruly and vicious character. He explained in the letter that he had spoken in this manner the better to win his case. He did not consider it yet won, but he would go to see him the next day and have another try. He concluded by saying that the young man should go to his house.

Damião finished reading the letter and glanced toward Sinhá Rita. She is my only hope, he thought. Sinhá Rita sent for her inkstand of carved horn, and on the same sheet of paper, below the letter itself, she wrote this reply: "Joãozinho, either you rescue the boy, or we never see each other again." She folded the paper and sealed it with wax, handed it to the slave, and told him to take it back with all speed. She returned to the job of cheering up the seminarist, for he was once more very low and shrouded in despair. She told him to rest easy and leave the matter to her.

"They'll find out what I'm made of!.No, I won't stand for any foolishness!"

It was now time to gather up the pieces of needle-work. Sinhá Rita inspected them. All the others had finished their tasks. Only Lucretia still sat before her cushion, moving the bobbins in and out, for some time now without seeing. Sinhá Rita came to where she sat, saw that the allotted task was not finished, became furious, and grabbed her by the ear.

"Ah! low-down good-for-nothing!"

"Nhanhã, Nhanhã,* for the love of God! by Our Lady that is in heaven!"

"Trashy good-for-nothing! Our Lady does not protect lazy-bones."

With a tremendous effort, Lucretia wrenched herself free from the hands of her mistress, and ran out of the room. The mistress went after her and grabbed her.

"Come back here!"

* Corruption of *senhora*.

"Mistress, forgive me!" coughed the little black girl.

"No, I won't forgive you! Where is the rod?"

They both came back into the sitting room: one held by the ear, struggling, crying, begging; the other saying "no," that she was going to punish her.

"Where is the rod?"

The rod lay on the floor by the settee, on the other side of the room. Sinhá Rita was unwilling to loose her hold on the little girl and yelled to the seminarist, "Senhor Damião, give me that rod, if you please!"

Damião froze . . . Cruel moment! A cloud passed before his eyes. Yes, he had sworn to protect the little girl; it was because of him that she was behind with her work . . .

"Give me the rod, Senhor Damião!"

Damião finally started to walk toward the settee. The little Negress begged him then by all he held most sacred, in the name of his mother, his father, of Our Lord . . .

"Help me, sweet young master!"

Sinhá Rita, her face on fire, her eyes starting from her head, kept calling for the rod, without letting go of the little black girl, who was now held in a fit of coughing.

Damião was pricked by an uneasy ∍nse of guilt, but he wanted so much to get out of the seminary! He reached the settee, picked up the rod, and handed it to Sinhá Rita.

Translated by HELEN CALDWELL

The Animal Game

Camillo—or Camillinho, as he was affectionately known to his friends—held a position as clerk in one of the arsenals of Rio de Janeiro (Army or Navy). He earned two hundred milreis a month, subject to tax and pension deductions. He was a bachelor, but once, during the holidays, he went to spend Christmas night at the home of a friend in the suburb of Rocha. There he saw a modest little thing, blue dress, appealing eyes. Three months later they were married.

Neither had anything. He, nothing more than his salary; she, her willing hands and energy to take care of the whole house, which was small, and help the old colored woman who had been her nurse and followed her without wages. It was this colored woman who made them get married all the sooner. Not that she gave them any such advice. As a matter of fact, it seemed better to her for the girl to remain with her widowed aunt, without either responsibilities or children. But no one asked her for her opinion. Since, however, she had one day said that if her baby married she would go and work for her without pay, this remark was told to Camillo, and Camillo made up his mind to get married two months later. If he had thought about it a little, perhaps he would not have married right away: the colored woman was old, they were young, and so forth. The idea that the colored woman would work for them without pay was entered as a permanent appropriation in his fiscal estimate.

Germana, the colored woman, was as good as her word. "This little old bag of bones can still cook up a pot of stew," she said.

A year later the couple had a child. And the joy it brought made up for the burdens it would bring. Joanninha, the wife, got along without a wet nurse; she had so much milk, was so

84

strong—not to mention the lack of money, and it is certain they never even thought of that.

The young clerk was all joy, all hope. There was going to be a reorganization at the arsenal, and he would be promoted. While the reorganization was slow in coming, there was a vacancy caused by death, and Camillo joined in his co-worker's funeral procession, almost laughing. At home he did not restrain himself and laughed aloud. He told his wife exactly what would happen, the name of those up for promotion—two, a certain Botelho, favored by General ——, and he. The promotions took place, and the choice lighted upon Botelho and another man. Camillo wept bitterly; he beat his fists into the bed, against the table, and himself.

"Have patience," said Joanninha.

"Patience! For five years I've just been marking time . . ." He broke off. That word, of military origin, used by an employee of the arsenal, was oil on troubled waters: it comforted him. Camillo was delighted with himself. He went so far as to repeat it to some of his close friends.

Not long after, when there was again talk of a reorganization, Camillo went to see the minister and said, "Look, Your Excellency, for more than five years now I have just been *marking time.*"

The italics are to convey the emphasis with which he uttered the final phrase. It seemed to him that it made a good impression on the minister, even though all the classes might use the same metaphor—bank clerks, tradesmen, judges, industrialists, and so on.

There was no reorganization: Camillo reconciled himself and went on living. He already had a few debts, was borrowing against his salary, and looking for odd jobs, secretly, on the outside. Since they were young, and in love, the bad weather only made them think of a sky that was everlastingly blue.

Even without this explanation, there was a whole week when Camillo's joy knew no bounds. You shall see. Let posterity hear me! It was when Camillo played the animals for the first time. "Playing the animals" is not a euphemism like "playing ducks and drakes." The player chooses a number that by established custom is identified with a certain animal, and if this number turns out to be the winning number in the lottery all who risked their pennies on it win, and all who placed their trust in other numbers and other animals lose. It began with pennies, and they say it is now up in the millions. But let us get on with our story.

For the first time, Camillo played the animals: he chose the monkey, and with a bet of five *tostões* won I do not know how many times as much. He found this so preposterous that he refused to believe it, but finally he had to believe it and go collect the money. Naturally, he tried the monkey again—two, three, four times—but this animal, half-human, did not live up to its early promise. Camillo threw himself on the mercy of other animals, with no better luck, and all the winnings went into the bookie's cash drawer. He saw it would be better to rest for a while. But there is no eternal rest, not even in the grave. One day, along comes an archaeologist digging up bones and eras.

Camillo had faith. And faith levels mountains. He tried the cat, then the dog, then the ostrich: since he had not bet on them it could be that . . . It could not be. Fortune scattered her favors impartially on all three animals: she saw to it that none of them paid. He was unwilling to follow the tips in the newspapers, as some of his friends did. Camillo asked how half a dozen news hacks could foretell the numbers of the grand prize. Once, to prove the error of their thinking, he agreed to follow a tip, bought on the cat, and won.

"Well?" said his friends.

"You can't always lose," he replied.

"You can end up always winning," said one of them. "It's a question of tenacity, of never weakening."

In spite of this, Camillo went on with his own system of calculations—though he sometimes gave way before certain signs that appeared to come from heaven, like something a child said in the street, "Mother, why don't you bet on the snake?" He would bet on the snake and lose, and explain the fact with the best reasoning in this world; and reason strengthens faith.

Instead of a reorganization in his department, there was an increase in salaries, about sixty *milreis* a month. Camillo decided to baptize his son, and chose as godfather no less a person than the very fellow who sold him the animals—his trusted "banker." There was no family connection between them. It even seems that the man was a bachelor without any relatives. The request was so unexpected that it almost made him laugh; but he saw the young man's earnestness, was honored at being asked, and accepted with pleasure.

"No call for full dress?"

"Full dress! A modest little affair."

"Nor a carriage?"

"Carriage . . ."

"Why bother with a carriage, eh?"

"Yes, we *could* walk. The church is not far, in the next street or so."

"Then let us walk."

People of discernment will have already perceived that Camillo's feeling was that the baptismal party should ride in a carriage. They will have also perceived from his hesitation and manner that the idea of letting the godfather pay for the carriage entered into that feeling, and that if the godfather was not going to pay for the carriage nobody was. The baptism took place, the godfather left a gift for his godchild and promised with a laugh that he would give him a "win" on the eagle.

This silly joke explains the father's choice of godfather. It was his suspicion that the bookmaker shared in the animals' good luck, and he wanted to bind himself to him with a spiritual tie. He did not play the eagle right off, "so as not to startle . . . fate," he said to himself. But he did not forget the promise, and one day he laughingly reminded the bookmaker, "*Compadre*, be sure to warn me when it's to be the eagle."

"The eagle?"

Camillo recalled his remark. The bookmaker burst into a loud laugh. "No, compadre," he said, "I can't foretell the winner. I was only joking. I wish I could give you a prize. The eagle pays, not usually, but it does pay."

"Then why has it never won for me?"

"That I don't know. I can't give advice, but I am inclined to think, compadre, that you don't have enough patience with an animal, you don't play with true constancy. You keep changing. That's the reason you've won only a few times. Tell me now, how many times have you won?"

"Off hand, I can't say. But I have it all written down in my notebook."

"Well, you just look, and you'll see that your whole trouble is in not sticking with the same animal for any length of time. Now, there's a colored man who has been betting on the butterfly for three months: yesterday he won and carried off a pile of money . . ."

Camillo really did keep a written account of his disbursements and receipts, but he never compared them—in order to remain in ignorance of the difference. He did not want to know the deficit. Though methodical, he had a genuine talent for closing his eyes to the truth, so as not to see it and be saddened by it. On the other hand, the suggestion made by his child's godfather was worth considering: perhaps his restlessness, impatience, and not sticking with the same animals was the reason for his never winning anything.

When he got home he found his wife divided between the kitchen and her sewing. Germana was sick in bed, Joanninha was cooking dinner and at the same time finishing a dress for one of her customers. She now took in sewing to help with the household expense and to buy an occasional dress for herself. The husband did not hide his dismay over the situation. He ran in to look at the colored woman. The fever had already gone down; his wife had given her some quinine she had in the house —on a "hunch." And the old colored woman added with a smile, "Nhã* Joanninha's hunches good."

He was sad as he sat down to dinner, at seeing his wife so burdened with work, but her gaiety in the face of everything soon put him in a gay mood too. After dinner he got out the notebook that he kept shut up in a drawer, and began to go over his accounts. He added up the bets and the animals: so many on the snake, so many on the cat, so many on the dog, and on the others—a complete fauna, but so lacking in persistence that it was easy to miss. He was reluctant to total the disbursements and the receipts because he did not want to receive a blow between the eyes, and closed the book. Finally he gave in and began to add the totals—slowly, carefully, so as not to make a mistake: he had spent seven hundred and seven milreis, and had won

* Corruption of *senhora.*

eighty-four milreis—a deficit of six hundred and twenty-three milreis. He was astounded.

"It's not possible!"

He added the columns a second time, still more slowly, and found the difference to be five milreis less. His hopes rose and he once more added up the amounts spent, and arrived at the original deficit of six hundred and twenty-three milreis. He shut the book up in the drawer. Joanninha, who had seen him gay and lively at dinner, was surprised at the change, and asked what was wrong.

"Nothing."

"Something's wrong. Something you remembered . . ."

"It wasn't anything."

As his wife insisted on knowing, he made up a story out of whole cloth—a set-to with the head of his department—a matter of no importance.

"But you were so gay . . ."

"That proves it's of no importance. Just now I happened to remember it . . . and was thinking about it, but it's nothing . . . How about a game of *bisca?*"

Bisca was their "show," their opera, their Rua do Ouvidor, Petropolis, Tijuca—everything that can convey the idea of amusement, outings, and pleasant idleness. The wife's gaiety returned. As for the husband, if he was not quite so expansive as usual, he found some pleasure, and great hope, in the numbers on the cards. As he played, he made calculations, on the basis of the first card dealt, then of the second, then the third; he waited for the last; he made other combinations, to see which animals would come up. And he saw a lot of them, but principally the monkey and the snake; it was in these he put his trust.

"My mind is made up," he concluded on the following day, "I will go as far as seven hundred milreis. If I don't win a good substantial amount by then, I won't bet any more."

He decided to place his trust in the snake, because of its wiliness, and set out in the direction of the godfather's place. He told him he had taken his advice and was going to start by sticking with the snake.

"The snake is a good one," said his child's godfather.

Camillo bet on the snake a whole week without winning a thing. On the seventh day he got the idea of mentally fixing on a certain species, and he chose the coral snake. It lost. The next day he called it a rattlesnake. It lost too. Then it became a twelve-foot bushmaster, a boa constrictor, a viper. None of the varieties escaped the same unhappy fortune. He changed his direction. He was quite capable of changing it without reason, in spite of his promise; but what actually made him do it was that he happened to see a carriage run over a poor little child. A crowd gathered, the police came, the child was taken to a pharmacy, the driver to the station. Camillo saw scarcely anything but the number on the carriage: its final digits were the same as the lamb's. He embraced the lamb. The lamb was no luckier than the snake.

Although Camillo had mastered the system of adopting an animal and betting on it until it was played out, he did not spurn the use of lucky numbers. For example, he would turn a corner with his eyes on the ground, take forty, sixty, eighty steps, suddenly raise his eyes and glance at the house on his right, or left, take down the number, and bet on the corresponding animal. He had already used up the combinations he had written down and placed in his hat, numbers on treasury notes—he rarely saw those any more—and a hundred other methods tried over and over again, or with slight variations. In every case, he always fizzled out into impatience and kept shifting back and forth. One day he made a resolution: he resolved to pin his faith to the lion, and stick by him. When his son's godfather realized that he had made up his mind not to abandon the king of beasts under any circumstance, he gave thanks to God.

"Well, thanks be to God that I should ever see you ready to take this great step. The lion has been disinclined of late, he'll probably knock over everything any day now."

"Disinclined? You don't mean to say . . . ?"

"On the contrary."

Say what? On the contrary what? Dark words, but, for one who has faith and deals with numbers, nothing plainer. Camillo increased the size of his bet. He had almost reached the seven hundred milreis: win or die!

The young wife kept up the cheerful gaiety of their home, however hard life might be, however rude her tasks, however fast their debts and borrowings grew, and the not infrequent times of hunger. The fault did not lie with her, but she was patient none the less. He, when he had lost the seven hundred milreis, would lock the barn door. The lion was unwilling to pay. Camillo considered trading it for another animal, but his child's godfather would become so upset at such weakness that he always ended up in the arms of royalty. The seven hundred milreis were running out, were almost gone.

"Today I can breathe freely," Camillo said to his wife. "This is the last time."

About two o'clock, as he sat at his desk in the government office, copying a serious and weighty document, Camillo's mind ran on numbers as he cursed Lady Luck. The document contained figures, and he kept making mistakes in them because of the stampede of digits in his brain. A slip was easy; the numbers from his brain turned up more often on the paper than those from the original document. And the worst of it was that he did not notice the mistake: he would write down the lion instead of transcribing the proper number of tons of gunpowder.

Suddenly, an errand boy came into the room, went up to Camillo and whispered in his ear that the lion had paid. Camillo dropped his pen; the ink ran out and spoiled the copy, which was almost finished. Under other circumstances it would have been reason to bring his fist down on the paper and break the pen, but the circumstances were these: the lion had paid. Paper and pen escaped the justest acts of violence in this world. The lion had paid. But, since doubt does not die:

"Who told you the lion paid?" Camillo asked in a whisper.

"The fellow who sold me a ticket on the snake."

"Then it was the snake that paid."

"No, senhor. He made a mistake. He came to notify me because he thought I bet on the lion, but it was on the snake."

"You're sure?"

"Positive."

Camillo decided to dash out of there right then, but the ink-blotted paper motioned him back. He went to the head of his department, told him of the mishap, and asked permission to copy it over the next day: he would come early, or take the original home . . .

"What are you talking about? The copy has to be got out today."

"But it's almost three o'clock."

"I'll postpone closing time."

Camillo would like to have postponed the department head into the sea, if such a use of the verb and of the regulation had been permissible. He went back to his desk, took a sheet of paper, and began to write his resignation. The lion had paid; he could send this life of hell to the devil. All this in rapid seconds, scarcely a minute and a half. Since he could not do otherwise, he began to recopy the document, and by four o'clock it was finished. The handwriting came out shaky and uneven—furiously angry, then melancholy, little by little lively and gay, as the lion kept repeating in the clerk's ear, in a softened voice, "I paid! I paid!"

"Well! Come here and give me a hug," said the baby's godfather when Camillo turned up at his place. "At last, Fortune has begun to show some regard for you."

"How much?"

"One hundred and five milreis."

Camillo got hold of himself and took the hundred and five milreis. Not until he was in the street did he remember he had not thanked his child's godfather; he stopped, hesitated, then went on. A hundred and five milreis! He was on fire to get home and tell his wife the good news; but like that . . . nothing more . . . ?

"Yes, one should celebrate this marvelous happening. Today is not just another day. I must give thanks to heaven for the fortune it has bestowed upon me. Something special for dinner . . ."

He saw a pastry shop close by, went in, and ran his eyes over the display without choosing anything. The shopkeeper came to help him, and as Camillo hung uncertain between a meat dish and dessert, decided to sell him both. He began with a meat pie, "a magnificent meat pie that would fill the eyes before it filled one's mouth and stomach." The dessert was "a magnificent pudding" on which was written in white confectionery this indestructible viva: "Long live hope!" Camillo's joy was so great and so evident that the man had no recourse but to suggest wine also—a bottle, or two. Two.

"This calls for port. I'll have a boy deliver it all to your house. It's not far, is it?"

Camillo agreed, and paid the bill. He gave directions to the boy about the address and what he should do. He should not knock at the door but wait outside for him. He might not yet be home. If he was, he would come to the window from time to time. He paid sixteen milreis and went out.

He was so happy with the dinner he was bringing home, and the surprise to his wife, that he never once thought of buying her a gift. This idea did not come to him until he was on the street car. He got off and went back on foot to look for some trinket or other, if only a little gold pin with a precious stone. He found just such a pin, so modest in price—fifty milreis—that he was astonished. He bought it, like that, and flew homeward.

When he arrived, the delivery boy was standing outside with the look of a boy that had already called him some bad names and sent him to the devil. He took the packages from him, and offered him a tip.

"No, senhor, the boss doesn't allow it."

"Then don't tell him. Here! Here's ten tostões. You can buy a ticket on the snake. Bet on the snake!"

His recommending the animal that had not paid, instead of the lion, which had paid, was not from calculation—or meanness. It was, quite likely, confusion. The boy took the ten tostões. Camillo went into the house, with the packages and his whole soul in his arms, and thirty-eight milreis in his pocket.

Translated by HELEN CALDWELL

Midnight Mass

I have never quite understood a conversation that I had with a lady many years ago, when I was seventeen and she was thirty. It was Christmas Eve. I had arranged to go to Mass with a neighbor and was to rouse him at midnight for this purpose.

The two-story house in which I was staying belonged to the notary Menezes, whose first wife had been a cousin of mine. His second wife, Conceição [Conception], and her mother had received me hospitably upon my arrival a few months earlier. I had come to Rio from Mangaratiba to study for the college entrance examinations. I lived quietly with my books. Few contacts. Occasional walks. The family was small: the notary, his wife, his mother-in-law, and two female slaves. An old-fashioned household. By ten at night everyone was in his bedroom; by half-past ten the house was asleep.

I had never gone to a theater and, more than once, on hearing Menezes say that he was going, I asked him to take me along. On these occasions his mother-in-law frowned and the slaves tittered. Menezes did not reply; he dressed, went out, and returned the next morning. Later I learned that the theater was a euphemism. Menezes was having an affair with a married woman who was separated from her husband; he stayed out once a week. Conceição had grieved at the beginning, but after a time she had grown used to the situation. Custom led to resignation, and finally she came almost to accept the affair as proper.

Gentle Conceição! They called her the saint and she merited the title, so uncomplainingly did she suffer her husband's neglect. In truth, she possessed a temperament of great equanimity, with extremes neither of tears nor of laughter. Everything about her was passive and attenuated. Her very face was median, neither pretty nor ugly. She was what is called a kind person. She spoke ill of no one, she pardoned everything. She didn't know how to hate; quite possibly she didn't know how to love.

On that Christmas Eve (it was 1861 or 1862) the notary was at theater. I should have been back in Mangaratiba, but I had decided to remain till Christmas to see a midnight Mass in the big city. The family retired at the usual hour. I sat in the front parlor, dressed and ready. From there I could leave through the entrance hall without waking anyone. There were three keys to the door: the notary had one, I had one, and one remained in the house.

"But Mr. Nogueira, what will you do all this while?" asked Conceição's mother.

"I'll read, Madame Ignacia."

I had a copy of an old translation of *The Three Musketeers,* published originally, I think, in serial form in *The Journal of Commerce.* I sat down at the table in the center of the room and, by the light of the kerosene lamp, while the house slept, mounted once more D'Artagnan's bony nag and set out upon adventure. In a short time I was completely absorbed. The minutes flew as they rarely do when one is waiting. I heard the clock strike eleven, but almost without noticing. After a time, however, a sound from the interior of the house roused me from my book. It was the sound of footsteps, in the hall that connected the parlor with the dining room. I raised my head. Soon I saw the form of Conceição appear at the door.

"Haven't you gone?" she asked.

"No, I haven't. I don't think it's midnight yet."

"What patience!"

Conceição, wearing her bedroom slippers, came into the room. She was dressed in a white negligee, loosely bound at the waist. Her slenderness helped to suggest a romantic apparition quite in keeping with the spirit of my novel. I shut the book. She sat on the chair facing mine, near the sofa. To my question whether perchance I had awakened her by stirring about, she quickly replied:

"No, I woke up naturally."

I looked at her and doubted her statement. Her eyes were not those of a person who had just slept. However, I quickly put out of my mind the thought that she could be guilty of lying. The

possibility that I might have kept her awake and that she might
have lied in order not to make me unhappy, did not occur to
me at the time. I have already said that she was a good person,
a kind person.

"I guess it won't be much longer now," I said.

"How patient you are to stay awake and wait while your
friend sleeps! And to wait alone! Aren't you afraid of ghosts? I
thought you'd be startled when you saw me."

"When I heard footsteps I was surprised. But then I soon saw
it was you."

"What are you reading? Don't tell me, I think I know: it's
The Three Musketeers."

"Yes, that's right. It's very interesting."

"Do you like novels?"

"Yes."

"Have you ever read *The Little Sweetheart?*"

"By Mr. Macedo? I have it in Mangaratiba."

"I'm very fond of novels, but I don't have much time for them.
Which ones have you read?"

I began to name some. Conceição listened, with her head resting on the back of her chair, looking at me past half-shut eyelids.
From time to time she wet her lips with her tongue. When I
stopped speaking she said nothing. Thus we remained for several
seconds. Then she raised her head; she clasped her hands and
rested her chin on them, with her elbows on the arms of her
chair, all without taking from me her large, perceptive eyes.

"Maybe she's bored with me," I thought. And then, aloud:
"Madame Conceição, I think it's getting late and I . . ."

"No, it's still early. I just looked at the clock; it's half-past
eleven. There's time yet. When you lose a night's sleep, can you
stay awake the next day?"

"I did once."

"I can't. If I lose a night, the next day I just have to take a
nap, if only for half an hour. But of course I'm getting on in
years."

"Oh, no, nothing of the sort, Madame Conceição!"

I spoke so fervently that I made her smile. Usually her gestures were slow, her attitude calm. Now, however, she rose suddenly, moved to the other side of the room, and, in her chaste

disarray, walked about between the window and the door of her husband's study. Although thin, she always walked with a certain rocking gait as if she carried her weight with difficulty. I had never before felt this impression so strongly. She paused several times, examining a curtain or correcting the position of some object on the sideboard. Finally she stopped directly in front of me, with the table between us. The circle of her ideas was narrow indeed: she returned to her surprise at seeing me awake and dressed. I repeated what she already knew, that I had never heard a midnight Mass in the city and that I didn't want to miss the chance.

"It's the same as in the country. All Masses are alike."

"I guess so. But in the city there must be more elegance and more people. Holy Week here in Rio is much better than in the country. I don't know about St. John's Day or St. Anthony's . . ."

Little by little she had leaned forward; she had rested her elbows on the marble top of the table and had placed her face between the palms of her hands. Her unbuttoned sleeves fell naturally, and I saw her forearms, very white and not so thin as one might have supposed. I had seen her arms before, although not frequently, but on this occasion sight of them impressed me greatly. The veins were so blue that, despite the dimness of the light, I could trace every one of them. Even more than the book, Conceição's presence had served to keep me awake. I went on talking about holy days in the country and in the city, and about whatever else came to my lips. I jumped from subject to subject, sometimes returning to an earlier one; and I laughed in order to make her laugh, so that I could see her white, shining, even teeth. Her eyes were not really black but were very dark; her nose, thin and slightly curved, gave her face an air of interrogation. Whenever I raised my voice a little, she hushed me.

"Softly! Mama may wake up."

And she did not move from that position, which filled me with delight, so close were our faces. Really there was no need to speak loudly in order to be heard. We both whispered, I more than she because I had more to say. At times she became serious, very serious, with her brow a bit wrinkled. After a while she tired and changed both position and place. She came around the table and sat on the sofa. I turned my head and could see the tips of her slippers, but only for as long as it took her to sit down: her negligee was long and quickly covered them. I remember that they were black. Conceição said very softly:

"Mama's room is quite a distance away, but she sleeps so lightly. If she wakes up now, poor thing, it will take her a long time to fall asleep again."

"I'm like that, too."

"What?" she asked, leaning forward to hear better.

I moved to the chair immediately next to the sofa and repeated what I had said. She laughed at the coincidence, for she, too, was a light sleeper, we were all light sleepers.

"I'm just like mama: when I wake up I can't fall asleep again. I roll all over the bed, I get up, I light the candle, I walk around, I lie down again, and nothing happens."

"Like tonight."

"No, no," she hastened.

I didn't understand her denial; perhaps she didn't understand it either. She took the ends of her belt and tapped them on her knees, or rather on her right knee, for she had crossed her legs. Then she began to talk about dreams. She said she had had only one nightmare in her whole life, and that one during her childhood. She wanted to know whether I ever had nightmares. Thus the conversation re-engaged itself and moved along slowly, continuously, and I forgot about the hour and about Mass. Whenever I finished a bit of narrative or an explanation she asked a question or brought up some new point, and I started talking again. Now and then she had to caution me.

"Softly, softly . . ."

Sometimes there were pauses. Twice I thought she was asleep. But her eyes, shut for a moment, quickly opened: they showed neither sleepiness nor fatigue, as though she had shut them merely so that she could see better. On one of these occasions I think she noticed that I was absorbed in her, and I remember that she shut her eyes again—whether hurriedly or slowly I do not remember. Some of my recollections of that evening seem abortive or confused. I get mixed up, I contradict myself. One thing I remember vividly is that at a certain moment she, who till then had been such engaging company (but nothing more), suddenly became beautiful, so very beautiful. She stood up, with her arms crossed. I, out of respect for her, stirred myself to rise;

she did not want me to, she put one of her hands on my shoulder, and I remained seated. I thought she was going to say something; but she trembled as if she had a chill, turned her back, and sat in the chair where she had found me reading. She glanced at the mirror above the sofa and began to talk about two engravings that were hanging on the wall.

"These pictures are getting old. I've asked Chiquinho to buy new ones."

Chiquinho was her husband's nickname. The pictures bespoke the man's principal interest. One was of Cleopatra; I no longer remember the subject of the other, but there were women in it. Both were banal. In those days I did not know they were ugly.

"They're pretty," I said.

"Yes, but they're stained. And besides, to tell the truth, I'd prefer pictures of saints. These are better for bachelors' quarters or a barber shop."

"A barber shop! I didn't think you'd ever been to . . ."

"But I can imagine what the customers there talk about while they're waiting—girls and flirtations, and naturally the proprietor wants to please them with pictures they'll like. But I think pictures like that don't belong in the home. That's what I think, but I have a lot of queer ideas. Anyway, I don't like them. I have an Our Lady of the Immaculate Conception, my patron saint; it's very lovely. But it's a statue, it can't be hung on the wall, and I wouldn't want it here anyway. I keep it in my little oratory."

The oratory brought to mind the Mass. I thought it might be time to go and was about to say so. I think I even opened my mouth but shut it before I could speak, so that I could go on listening to what she was saying, so sweetly, so graciously, so gently that it drugged my soul. She spoke of her religious devotions as a child and as a young girl. Then she told about dances and walks and trips to the island of Paquetá, all mixed together, almost without interruption. When she tired of the past she spoke of the present, of household matters, of family cares, which, before her marriage, everyone said would be terrible, but really they were nothing. She didn't mention it, but I knew she had been twenty-seven when she married.

She no longer moved about, as at first, and hardly changed position. Her eyes seemed smaller, and she began to look idly about at the walls.

"We must change this wallpaper," she said, as if talking to herself.

I agreed, just to say something, to shake off my magnetic trance or whatever one may call the condition that thickened my tongue and benumbed my senses. I wished and I did not wish to end the conversation. I tried to take my eyes from her, and did so out of respect; but, afraid she would think I was tired of looking at her, when in truth I was not, I turned again towards her. The conversation was dying away. In the street, absolute stillness.

We stopped talking and for some time (I cannot say how long) sat there in silence. The only sound was the gnawing of a rat in the study; it stirred me from my somnolescence. I wanted to talk about it but didn't know how to begin. Conceição seemed to be abstracted. Suddenly I heard a beating on the window and a voice shouting:

"Midnight Mass! Midnight Mass!"

"There's your friend," she said, rising. "It's funny. You were to wake him, and here he comes to wake you. Hurry, it must be late. Goodbye."

"Is it time already?"

"Of course."

"Midnight Mass!" came the voice from outside, with more beating on the window.

"Hurry, hurry, don't make him wait. It was my fault. Goodbye until tomorrow."

And with her rocking gait Conceição walked softly down the hall. I went out into the street and, with my friend, proceeded to the church. During Mass, Conceição kept appearing between me and the priest; charge this to my seventeen years. Next morning at breakfast I spoke of the midnight Mass and of the people I had seen in church, without, however, exciting Conceição's interest. During the day I found her, as always, natural, benign, with nothing to suggest the conversation of the prior evening.

A few days later I went to Mangaratiba. When I returned to Rio in March, I learned that the notary had died of apoplexy. Conceição was living in the Engenho Novo district, but I neither visited nor met her. I learned later that she had married her husband's apprenticed clerk.

Translated by WILLIAM L. GROSSMAN

Father versus Mother

Slavery brought with it its own trades and tools, as happens no doubt with any social institution. If I mention certain tools, it is only because they are linked to a certain trade. One of them was the iron collar, another the leg iron. There was also the mask of tin plate.

The mask cured slaves of the vice of drunkenness by sealing up their mouths. It had three holes, two to see through, one for breathing, and it was fastened behind the head with a lock and chain. Along with the vice of drinking they lost the temptation to steal, because, usually, it was with pennies stolen from their master that they killed their thirst: here were two sins wiped out at once, and sobriety and honesty assured. It was grotesque, this mask! But a humane social order is not always achieved without the grotesque, and sometimes not without the cruel. The tin-smiths had them hung up for sale at the doors of their shops. But let us not concern ourselves with masks.

The iron collar was used for runaway slaves. Imagine a thick dog collar made of iron with a projecting iron shaft, on the right or left, clear to the top of the head. It too was locked on with a key. It was heavy probably, but it was less a punishment than an identification. A runaway slave wearing such a collar, no matter where he went, showed that he was a hardened offender, and was easily caught.

A half-century ago, slaves ran away frequently. There were many slaves, and not all of them liked slavery. It happened sometimes that they were beaten, and not all of them liked being beaten. A great part of them were only scolded: there would be someone in the household who acted as their sponsor, and the owner himself was not always mean; besides, the feeling of ownership moderated his actions, because money hurts too. Running away continued nevertheless. There were instances, though they may have been rare, in which the contraband slave, just bought at the smugglers' market in Vallongo, would take off at a run without even knowing the streets of the city. The cleverer ones followed along peaceably to the house, where they asked the master to set a price on their daily service, and went out and earned it peddling in the streets.

A man whose slave ran away would give a small sum to anyone bringing him back. He would put notices in the papers, with a description of the runaway, his name, clothes, physical defect, if he had one, the neighborhood where he had been, and the amount of the reward. When the amount was not given, a promise was: "will be generously rewarded," or "will receive a handsome reward." Many times, the notice had above it, or to one side, a vignette of a black figure, barefoot, running, with a pole over his shoulder and a bundle on the end of it. And it threatened to prosecute to the full measure of the law anyone who beat him.

Catching runaway slaves, you see, was one of the trades of the time. It may not have been a noble calling, but, as an instrument of the force by which law and property rights are maintained, it had that other nobility attaching to the vindication of private ownership. No one followed this trade out of a liking for it, or because he had been trained to it. Poverty, the need for a little extra cash, unfitness for other work, chance, and, occasionally, a natural taste for serving, though in a different way, supplied the incentive to a man who felt firm enough to reduce disorder and distress to a system.

Candido Neves—Candinho to his family—is the person involved in this story of a runaway. He yielded to poverty when he took up the trade of catching slaves. This man had a serious defect: he could not stick to a job or trade. He lacked stability; he called it "hard luck." He began by deciding to learn printing but he soon saw that it would take some time to become a good compositor, and, even so, most likely he would not earn enough. That is what he told himself. Commerce next attracted him, it was a fine career. With a little effort he got a job clerking in a haberdashery. The obligation, however, slavishly to wait on everyone and anyone offended his pride. At the end of five or six weeks he was, by his own volition, out of a job. Cashier in a registry office, messenger in a subdepartment of the Imperial Ministry, sales clerk, and other positions were left shortly after they had been obtained.

Then came the moment when he fell in love with Clara. He had nothing, except debts—though not so many of those either, because he lived with a cousin, a woodcarver by trade. After several attempts to obtain a job he decided to follow his cousin's trade, especially since the cousin had already given him a few lessons. It was a simple matter to obtain more. But, in his desire to learn quickly, he learned badly. He was not making delicate or complicated pieces, only clawed feet for sofas and simple raised decorations on chairs. He wanted something to work at when he married, and marriage was not far off, as it turned out.

He was thirty, Clara twenty-two. She was an orphan, lived with her aunt Monica. The two women took in sewing for a living. Clara did not do so much sewing that she did not have time for a little flirting. But her admirers only wanted to kill time; they had no further thought. They would come by in the afternoons, ogle her and she them, till night made her go in to her sewing. She had noticed that none of them caused her any yearning or kindled any spark of passion in her. Perhaps she did not even know the name of many of them. Naturally she had marriage in mind. It was, as her aunt told her, fishing with a pole to see if the fish would bite. But the fish went by at some distance. If one stopped, it was only to circle the bait, eye it, smell it, leave it, and go on to other tempting hooks.

Love comes in an envelope with a name and address on it. When the young woman saw Candido Neves she felt that he could be her husband, her true, her only husband. The meeting occurred at a dance: it was—to recall the young man's former trade—the first page of that book, which was to leave the press badly printed and with a worse binding. The wedding took place eleven months later, and was the finest celebration the young couple's relatives had ever enjoyed. Some of Clara's friends, less out of friendship than from envy, tried to hold her back from the step she was taking. They did not deny the gentle manners of her betrothed, nor the love he bore her, nor even one or two virtues; they said he was too much given to fun and parties.

"All the better," answered the bride. "At least I'm not marrying a corpse."

"No, not a corpse! It's simply that . . ."

They did not say what. After the marriage, in the poor little house where the couple and the aunt had taken shelter, Aunt Monica did, one day, bring up the possibility of children. They wanted a child, just one, even if it should aggravate their poverty.

"If you two have a baby," the aunt said to her niece, "you'll die of hunger."

"Our Lady in heaven will feed us," retorted Clara.

Aunt Monica ought to have given the advice, or warning, when Candido came to ask for the girl's hand, but she too was fond of fun and parties, and the wedding was sure to be a big celebration—as it was!

All three of them were happy. The newlyweds laughed at everything. Even their names were the objects of puns: Clara (bright), Neves (snow), Candido (white). They did not produce food, but they produced laughter, and laughter is digested without effort. She sewed more now; he worked at odd jobs, at one thing and another, but had nothing certain.

Even so, they did not give up the hope of a child. But the child, not knowing of this specific wish, allowed itself to remain hidden in eternity. One day, however, it made itself known. Male or female, it was the blessed fruit that would bring the couple their longed-for fortune. Aunt Monica was dismayed. Candido and Clara laughed at her fears.

"God will help us, auntie," insisted the mother-to-be.

The word ran through the neighborhood. There was nothing more to do but wait for the dawn of the great day. The wife was now working with a will, and it was necessary to do so, seeing that besides sewing for others she had to make clothes for the baby, out of the scraps. Constantly thinking of it, she came to live with it, as she measured its diapers, its little shirts. The scraps, and the pay, were meager, the times between long. Aunt Monica helped, you may be certain, though not without grumbling.

"It's a sad life you'll have," she sighed.

"But aren't other children born?" asked Clara.

"They are, and they are always certain of something to eat, even if it is very little . . ."

"Certain of something . . ."

"Certain . . . a job, a trade, but what does the father of this unhappy child waste his time at?"

As soon as Candido Neves learned of the aunt's remark, he went straight to her. He was not rude to her, but still much less gentle than usual. He asked if there had ever been a day when she had not eaten.

"You have never fasted, senhora, except during Holy Week, and then it was because you did not choose to dine at my table. We have never gone without our codfish . . ."

"I know, but we are three."

"We shall be four."

"It's not the same thing."

"What would you have me do, more than I am doing?"

"Something more certain. Look at the carpenter on the corner, the fellow in the haberdashery, the printer who got married Saturday, all of them have a job that's certain . . . Don't be angry! I don't say you are a loafer, but the occupation you have chosen . . . it's not steady. You go for weeks without making a cent."

"Yes, but then there comes a night that makes up for everything, and more. God will not forsake me, and runaway slaves know I'm not to be trifled with. Almost none of them put up a fight, many give themselves up at once." He prided himself on this, and talked of hope as if it were actual capital in the bank. In a few minutes he was laughing, and he had the aunt laughing too. She was of a naturally happy disposition, and foresaw a party in the baptism.

Candido Neves had abandoned the trade of woodcarver, as he had given up many other vocations, better and worse. Catching runaway slaves held a novel charm for him. It did not oblige him to remain seated for long hours together. All it required was strength, a quick eye, patience, daring, and a piece of rope. He would read the notices, copy them out, put them in his pocket, and sally forth to the search. He had a good memory. With the physical appearance and the habits of a slave firmly in mind, he lost little time in finding him, seizing him, binding him, and taking him to his owner. Strength was the big thing, agility too. More than once, as he stood on a street corner, talking of other matters, he would see a slave go by, like other slaves, and would know at once that he was running away, who he was, his name, owner, the latter's address and the amount of the reward: he would interrupt his conversation and go after the criminal. He would not grab him immediately, but would wait for the right place and moment, then with one leap the reward was in his hands. He did not always come out of it without loss of blood, the slave's nails and teeth went into action, but generally he took them without a scratch.

And then, the profits began to fall off. Runaway slaves no longer came and thrust themselves into the hands of Candido Neves. There were new, skillful hands. As the business grew, more than one unemployed fellow upped and got himself a rope, went to the newspaper offices, copied down the advertisements, and joined the hunt. He had more than one competitor right in his own neighborhood. That is to say, Candido Neves' debts began to mount, and there were none of those prompt, or almost prompt, repayments as formerly. Life became hard and painful, food was scarce and poor, they did not eat regularly. The landlord sent for the back rent.

Clara scarcely had time to mend her husband's clothing, so great was the necessity to sew for money. Aunt Monica helped her niece of course. When Neves came home in the afternoon they would see by his face that he had not earned a penny. He would have dinner and go out again in search of some runaway. It even happened, though not often, that he made a mistake and grabbed a faithful slave who was going about his master's business: such was the blindness of necessity. On a certain occasion, he seized a Negro who was free; he melted into a thousand apologies, but did not escape a pommeling at the hands of the man's relatives.

"That's all you needed!" exclaimed Aunt Monica when she saw him come in the door. And after she had heard about his mistake and its consequences, she added, "Give it up, Candinho. Find some other way of earning a living, some other job."

As a matter of fact, Candido would like to have done something else. Not for the reason suggested by Aunt Monica, but for the simple pleasure of changing his trade. It would be a way of changing his skin, or his personality. The trouble was he did not know of a business he could learn fast.

Nature continued on her way, the fetus grew, became a burden to its mother before it was born. It was the eighth month,

month of trouble and privation, less so, however, than the ninth, the narration of which I will also dispense with. It is better to tell only the outcome: it could not have been more bitter.

"No, Aunt Monica!" shouted Candinho, refusing a piece of advice, which it is painful for me to write—how much more painful for the father to hear! "Never! I will never do it!"

It was in the final week of that last, terrible, month that Aunt Monica advised the couple to carry the child that was soon to be born to the Wheel of abandoned babies.° There could not have been a word harder for two young parents to hear, when they were waiting on tiptoe for their child, to kiss it, watch over it, see it laugh, grow, grow fat, skip about . . . Abandon? What did she mean abandon? Candinho stared at her, and ended by bringing his fist down on the dining table. The table, which was old, and weak in the joints, almost collapsed. Clara interposed.

"Auntie doesn't mean any harm, Candinho."

"Harm?" retorted Aunt Monica. "Harm or good, no matter what I mean, I say it's the best thing you can do. You owe everybody. The meat and beans are giving out. If some money isn't coming in, how can a family grow? And besides, there's time. Later, when you have a more secure livelihood, sir, the children that are born will be received with the same love as this one, or with greater love. This one will be well brought up, will not want for anything. After all, the Wheel isn't a barren coast, is it, or a refuse dump? No one gets killed there, no one dies there without good reason, while here it is certain to die, living on next to nothing. After all . . ."

Aunt Monica finished the sentence with a shrug of her shoulders, turned, and went into her bedroom. She had hinted at this solution before, but this was the first time she had done it with such frankness and spirit—such cruelty, if you like. Clara stretched out her hand to her husband, as if to brace his courage. Candinho made a wry face and, under his breath, called the aunt "crazy."

The tenderness of the young couple was interrupted by someone knocking at the street door.

"Who is it?" called the husband.

"It's I."

° Turn box in the wall of a foundling hospital in which an infant was placed.

It was the landlord, who was a creditor for three months' rent. He had come in person to threaten his tenant. The latter asked him to come in.

"There's no need . . ."

"Please!"

The creditor came in but refused to sit down. He glanced around at the furniture to see what it would bring. He concluded, very little. He said he had come for the back rent, he did not expect more; but if it was not paid within five days he would put him out in the street. He had not worked hard just for the pleasure of keeping others in luxury. To look at him no one would say he was a property owner, but his words made up for what was lacking in his appearance, and poor Candido Neves preferred to keep still rather than make any reply. He inclined his head in a gesture at once of promise and of supplication. The landlord did not give an inch.

"Five days, or out you go," he repeated, putting his hand on the latch, and he left.

Candinho left by another door. In such crises he never reached the point of despair. He counted on a loan. He did not know how he would get it, or from whom, but he counted on it. He also went and checked the notices of runaway slaves. There were a number of them, some old, ones he had already looked for without success. He spent several hours to no purpose, and went back home. At the end of four days, he still had not been able to lay his hands on the cash. He tried to get influential backing, he went to people on good terms with the landlord, but all he got was a notice to move.

The situation was acute. They could not find a house. They did not count on anyone lending them one, they would be out in the street. They did not count on their aunt. Aunt Monica had the cleverness to obtain lodgings for the three of them at the home of a rich old lady who was willing to lend them the use of some rooms under her house, in back of the stable, on an inner court. Aunt Monica had the even greater cleverness to say nothing about it to the young couple, so that Candido Neves, in desperation over the crisis, would begin by abandoning his baby and would end by getting some sure, regular way of earning a living—would mend his ways, in short. She listened to Clara's complaints, without joining in, it is true, but without consoling her either. On the day they had to move she would astonish them with the news of the old lady's kindness, and they would have a better place to sleep than they had hoped.

That is what happened. Put out of their house, they went straight to the lodgings that had been lent them, and two days afterward the baby was born. The father's joy was tremendous, his wretchedness too. Aunt Monica insisted they place the baby on the Wheel.

"If you don't want to take it yourself, let me do it. I'll go to the Rua dos Barbonos."

Candido Neves begged her not to go, to wait, he would take it himself.

Please note, it was a boy, and both parents had wanted that sex. They had just nursed it, but, as it happened to be raining that night, the father said he would take it to the Wheel the following night.

He spent the rest of the evening going over his notes on runaway slaves. The rewards for the most part were in the form of vague promises. A few mentioned the exact amount—niggardly sums. One, however, came to a hundred milreis. It was for a mulatto woman. There was a description of her looks and clothing. Candido Neves had hunted for her without success, and had given up; he imagined some lover was hiding her. Now, though, the sight of the amount and the need for it stimulated him to one last, great effort.

He went out the next morning to look and make inquiries all along the Rua da Carioca and its square, along the Rua do Parto and the Rua da Ajuda, where she had last been seen according to the notice. He did not find her. Only a pharmacist, on the Rua da Ajuda, remembered selling an ounce of a certain drug, three days before, to a person who fitted the description. Candido Neves spoke as if he were the owner of the slave and courteously thanked the man for the information. He had no better luck with other runaways for whom the reward was uncertain or cheap.

He went home to the wretched quarters that had been lent them. Aunt Monica herself had prepared a meal for the young mother, and had the baby ready to be carried to the Wheel. The father, in spite of the agreement, could scarcely hide his grief at the spectacle. He refused to eat what Aunt Monica had kept for him. He said he was not hungry, and it was the truth. He thought of a thousand ways to save his son from the Wheel. None of them were worth anything. He could not forget the cave they were living in. He spoke to his wife, who proved to be resigned. Aunt Monica had painted for her what the baby's life would be with them: it would mean greater poverty, most likely the child would be doomed to die. Candido Neves had to keep his promise. He asked his wife to give their son the last milk it would drink at its mother's breast. This done, the baby fell asleep, the father picked it up and went out in the direction of the Rua dos Barbonos.

That he thought more than once of turning back with it is certain. It is no less certain that he hugged it to him, that he kissed it, that he covered its face to keep off the night air. As he turned into the Rua da Guarda Velha, he began to slacken his step.

"I will give it to them as late as possible," he murmured.

But, since the street did not stretch to infinity, or even for a long distance, he was bound to come to the end of it. It was then it occurred to him to go by way of one of the alleys that link that street to the Rua da Ajuda. When he reached the end of the alley and was going to turn to the right in the direction of the Largo da Ajuda, he saw the shadowy figure of a woman just opposite. It was the runaway mulatto. I will not describe Candinho's commotion because I could not do it justice. Let one adjective suffice, let us just say it was tremendous. Since the woman was going down the street, he, too, went down the street. A few steps away was the pharmacy where he had obtained the information I mentioned above. He went in, found the druggist, asked him if he would be so kind as to watch the baby for a minute: he would be back without fail.

"But . . ."

Candido Neves did not give him time to say anything, he dashed out, crossed the street to reach a place where he could grab the woman without raising an alarm. At the end of the street, when she was about to turn into the Rua de São José, he came closer. It was she, it was the runaway mulatto woman.

"Arminda!" he called; that was the name given in the advertisement.

She turned around, never suspecting anything. It was only when he took the rope out of his pocket and grabbed her arms that the poor slave girl understood and tried to get away. By then, it was impossible. With his powerful hands Candido Neves tied her wrists. He told her to keep on walking. She was going to scream, and even uttered one rather loud cry, when she suddenly realized no one would come to set her free, but quite the contrary. She begged him then to let her go, for the love of God.

"I'm pregnant, dear master!" she cried. "If your honor has a child, I beg you, for love of him, to let me go. I will be your slave, I will serve you as long as you like. Le' me go dear young master! Le' me go!"

"Don't keep me waiting! Get along!"

There was a struggle then, because the slave pulled back, moaning, dragging herself and her unborn child. Anyone passing by or standing in the door of a shop understood what it was and naturally did not come to the rescue. Arminda told Candinho that her master was very mean and probably would have her beaten with whips, and in her condition it would hurt much more. Yes, he would certainly order her to be whipped.

"You're the one to blame. Who told you to go having babies and then go running away?" he asked. He was in no joking mood, because of his baby that was back there in the pharmacy, waiting for him. It is certain too, he was not in the habit of making big speeches. He kept on pulling the slave woman down the Rua dos Ourives toward the Rua da Alfândega, where her master's house was. On the corner of that street, her struggling increased: she set her feet against the wall of a house and pulled back with great strength, but it was useless. All she gained was a few minutes delay in reaching the house, already close at hand. Finally she reached it—dragged, desperate, gasping for breath. Even there she went down on her knees, but in vain. The master was at home and came running to the rescue at the noise and the shouting of his name.

"Here's your runaway," said Candido Neves.

"It's she all right."

"My dear master!"

"Come on, come in . . ."

Arminda fell in the entrance. Her master opened his billfold and took out the hundred-milreis reward. Candido Neves put away the two fifty-milreis notes while the master again told the slave to come in. There, on the ground where she had fallen, driven by fear and pain, and after some struggle, she aborted. The fruit of some months came into this world without life, between the groans of its mother and the despairing gestures of its owner. Candido Neves saw the whole spectacle. He did not know what time it was. Whatever the hour, it was urgent that he run straight to the Rua da Ajuda, and that is what he did, without caring to know the outcome.

When he reached the pharmacy he found the druggist alone and no sign of the baby. Candido Neves was ready to strangle him. Fortunately the man explained everything in time. The baby was inside with the druggist's family, and they both went back there. The father took his son with the same passionate fury with which he had grasped the runaway slave a short time before— a different kind of fury of course, a fury of love. He mumbled a few words of thanks and hastily left—not in the direction of the Wheel of abandoned babies, but in the direction of the borrowed lodgings—with his son, and the reward of a hundred milreis.

Aunt Monica forgave him for bringing back the child, after she heard the explanation, seeing that he brought a hundred milreis with him. It is true, she did have some hard things to say against the slave woman because of her abortion, as well as for running away.

Candido Neves showered his son with kisses and with tears, and blessed the slave for running away. He did not give a hang about the abortion.

"Not all babies have the luck to be born!" Those were the words his heart beat out to him.

Translated by HELEN CALDWELL

Education of a Stuffed Shirt

A Dialogue

"Are you sleepy?"

"No, sir."

"Nor I. Let's talk a while. Open the window. What time is it?"

"Eleven."

"The last guest has left. Our modest little dinner is over. And so, my fine young gentleman, you have reached your twenty-first birthday. It was twenty-one years ago you first saw the light, on the fifth of August, 1854, a puny little nothing; and now you are a man, with an enormous moustache, and love affairs . . ."

"Aw, papa . . ."

"Don't pretend to be modest. Let us speak frankly and seriously, man to man. Close that door. I have some important things to say to you. Sit down. Let's talk."

"Twenty-one years of age, some stocks and bonds, a college degree: you can enter parliament, get a judgeship, go into the newspaper business, farming, industry, commerce, letters, the arts . . . An infinite number of careers are open to you. Twenty-one, my boy, is scarcely the first syllable of our destiny. Even Pitt and Napoleon, in spite of their precocity, were not much at twenty-one. But, whatever the profession of your choice, I want you to be great and illustrious, or at least known in the better circles. Lift yourself above the ordinary level of obscurity. Life, Janjão, is an enormous lottery: the prizes are few, the failures innumerable. Out of the sighs of one generation are kneaded the hopes of the next. That's life. There can be no wailing and cursing, but only taking things as they are, with their jobs and perquisites, their glories and indignities, and go bravely on."

"Yes, sir."

"Still, just as it is good thrift to put something by for a rainy day, so it is good social sense to provide oneself with a special craft or calling—in case the others fall through or do not sufficiently repay the efforts of our ambition. This is the advice I give you on the day of your majority."

"Believe me, I'm much obliged; but what calling? Won't you suggest one?"

"No calling, in my opinion, is more useful, more generally acceptable, than that of stuffed shirt. To be a stuffed shirt was the dream of my youth. I lacked, however, a father's guidance; and I end up as you see, with no other consolation or moral eminence than the hopes I deposit in you. Listen carefully, my boy, to what I say, and lay it to heart.

"You are young, and naturally have the fire, the exuberance, the impulsiveness of youth. Don't try to get rid of these traits but moderate them, so that at forty-five you can enter frankly and openly into the practice of correctness and the measured tread. The wise man who said, 'Gravity is a mysterious carriage of the body,' defined the decorum of the stuffed shirt. Do not confuse this gravity with that other gravity which, though it, too, may be present in the outer aspect, is a mere reflection or emanation of the mind. The gravity I have reference to is of the body, only of the body—a natural oddity or an acquired knack. As for the age of forty-five . . ."

"Yes, why forty-five?"

"Forty-five is not, as you may think, an arbitrary limit, born of pure caprice; it is the normal date for the phenomenon to occur. As a rule, the genuine stuffed shirt begins to manifest himself between the ages of forty-five and fifty, although some types appear between fifty-five and sixty—but these are rare. There is too the forty-year variety, and others still more precocious that blossom at thirty-five, and at thirty; they are not, however, at all common. I won't mention the twenty-five year kind: such early blooming is the privilege of genius."

"I see."

"But let us get to the heart of the matter. Once entered on this career you must exercise great caution in the choice of ideas you nourish in respect to others, and to yourself. The best thing will be not to have any. Something you will easily understand if you imagine, for example, an actor deprived of the use of an arm. He can, by a miracle of artistic cunning, conceal the defect from the eyes of the front rows, but it would be much better for him to have two arms. The same thing happens with ideas. It is possible by exercising inhuman restraint to smother them, hide them, till the day of your death; but even this talent is no ordinary one, and such continuous effort is not compatible with a normal life."

"But whatever gave you the idea that I . . ."

"You, my son, if I'm not mistaken, are endowed with the perfect mental inadequacy so necessary to the practice of this noble calling. I do not refer so much to the fidelity with which you repeat in a drawing room the opinions you heard on a street corner, and vice versa, because such behavior, though it indicates a certain want of ideas, might be no more than a slip of memory. No, I refer to the correct and precise gesture with which you draw yourself to your full height and frankly express your feelings in respect to the cut of a vest, the dimensions of a hat, the squeaking or silence of a pair of shoes. Here we have an eloquent symptom, here is something to pin one's hopes on. Since it may be that with age you will come to be afflicted with some ideas of your own, it is urgent that you equip and strengthen your mind. Ideas by their very nature are spontaneous and take one by surprise. No matter how we curb them they break loose and charge off headlong. Hence the sureness with which the mob, whose nose is extremely delicate in these matters, distinguishes the accomplished stuffed shirt from the amateur."

"I'm sure you're right, but this obstacle seems insurmountable."

"No, it isn't. There is a way. You must throw yourself into a systematic course of mind enfeeblement, read textbooks of rhetoric, listen to certain speeches, et cetera. Gin rummy, dominoes, and whist are approved remedies. Whist also possesses the rare advantage of schooling one to silence, and silence is circumspection in its most marked form. I do not say the same of swimming, horseback riding, and gymnastics, although it is true they keep the brain inactive. But, for that very reason, they rest it and restore its lost strength and power. The game of billiards is excellent."

"How so, if it, too, is a bodily exercise?"

"I don't say it isn't, but there are things in which actual observation disproves theory. If, by way of exception, I prescribe billiards, it is because the most scrupulously exact statistics show that three fourths of the devotees of the cue share the opinions of the same cue. A walk along the street, especially on streets given over to fashionable amusement and parade is most beneficial provided you don't go unaccompanied, because solitude is a factory for ideas, and the mind, left to itself, even in the midst of a crowd, will take on a certain amount of activity."

"But suppose I don't have the right kind of friend handy to go with me?"

"It doesn't signify. You have the manly recourse of mingling with idlers in the public lounging places, where all the dust of solitude blows away. Bookshops, either because of the atmosphere of the place, or for some other reason that eludes me, are not suited to our purpose. And yet there is great advantage in going into them from time to time. I don't mean stealthily, but openly, publicly. You can get around the difficulty in a simple manner: go there to talk about the rumor of the day, the story of the week, a shady deal, a scandal, a comet, anything—whenever you do not prefer to question directly the constant readers of *Time Magazine*'s glorious columns. Seventy-five per cent of these estimable gentlemen will give you verbatim the same opinions, and such monotony is eminently salutary. By following this regimen for eight, ten, eighteen months, say even two years, you will reduce your intellect, no matter how capacious it was to start with, to sobriety, control, and a well-tempered vulgarity. I do not touch upon vocabulary because it is really included under the heading 'ideas.' Naturally it must be simple, colorless, thin— there must be no dashes of crimson, no trumpet blasts . . ."

"That'll be hell! Not to be able to dress up one's style once in a while . . ."

"But you can. You can use any number of expressive tropes: the Lernean Hydra, for example, Medusa's head, the sieve of the Danaids, the flight of Icarus, and others that Romanticists, Classicists, and Naturalists employ without loss of reputation when they need them. Then there are Latin mottoes, historic remarks, famous quotations, legal saws, maxims . . . It's a good idea to have these ready to hand for after-dinner speeches, congratulatory remarks, and 'brief words' of acknowledgment. *Caveant consules* is an excellent close for a political article. I would say the same of *si vis pacem, para bellum,* 'if you want peace, prepare for war.' Some people have a way of freshening up the flavor of a quotation by working in a new, original, and handsome phrase, but I do not advise it: it means denaturing the quotation's time-honored charm.

"Yet, better than all this, which, in the long run, is nothing but trimming, are the stock phrases, the conventional expressions, the formulas consecrated by the years, incrusted on individual and public memory. Such phrases have the advantage of not obligating others to a needless effort. I won't recite them all now; I'll make a list of them for you later. Besides, the career of stuffed shirt itself will gradually teach you the elements of this difficult art of thinking what has been thought. As to the usefulness of the practice, just take a hypothetical case. A law is formulated, enacted, and has no effect: the evil persists. Here you have a question to whet idle curiosity, to give rise to an investigation by experts, with a tedious heap of documents and observations, analysis of probable causes, known causes, possible causes, an endless study of the capacities of the individual subject of the reform, of the nature of the evil, the preparation of the remedy, the circumstances of its application—matter, in short, for a whole scaffolding of words, opinions, and silly capers. *You* spare your fellow men all this immense rigmarole: you say simply, 'Rather than the laws, let us reform our customs!' And this concise, transparent, limpid phrase, drawn from the common fund, instantly solves the problem, entering into men's minds like a sudden burst of sunlight."

"I see by this that you, sir, condemn all and every application of modern processes."

"Let's not beat about the bush. I condemn them in practice; I praise them in name. The same goes for all the recent scientific terminology: you should get it by heart. Although the distinguishing characteristic of the stuffed shirt is a certain attitude of God Terminus, and the sciences on the other hand are a product of human push and bustle, still, since you are to be a stuffed shirt later on, it is best to adopt the weapons of your generation. Because one of two things will happen: either they will be worn out and common property thirty years from now, or they will remain shiny new. In the first instance they will rightfully belong to you as the natural prerogative of a stuffed shirt; in the second, you can wear them with a dapper air to show that 'you too are a painter.' From scraps of hearsay and random talk you will eventually pick up a vague notion of the cases and phenomena all this terminology fits, because the method of getting information directly from scientific experts and professors in their books, studies, and notes, besides being tedious, involves the danger of inoculating you with new ideas, and is basically wrong. There is an added danger that on the day you succeed in mastering the spirit of those laws and formulas you will be tempted to use them with a certain discretion, like the shrewd and prosperous dress-maker, who according to a classic poet,

> 'The more cloth she has the more she skimps
>   in the cutting
> And the smaller the pile of scraps left over.'

And such a procedure in the case of a stuffed shirt, would not be at all scientific."

"My word! What a difficult profession!"

"And we're not through yet."

"Let's go on then!"

"I haven't yet mentioned the advantages of publicity. Publicity is an imperious and demanding mistress that you must woo with a host of little trinkets, comfits, cushions for her back, tri-fling attentions that betoken the constancy of your affection rather than the boldness and ambition of your desire. Let Don Quixote solicit her favors by dint of heroic or painfully expensive gestures. It is a fit and proper vice for that illustrious lunatic. The stuffed shirt is of another school. Instead of composing *A scientific treatise on the breeding of sheep,* he buys one and presents it to his friends in the form of a dinner—a newspaper notice of which cannot be a matter of indifference to his fellow citizens. One notice prompts another, and places your name before the eyes of the world five, ten, twenty times. Committees or delegations to wait upon a person who has been given a medal, upon a public benefactor, or a foreign visitor are of inestimable value. The same is true of the various clubs and societies, whether they are devoted to mythology, venery, or terpsichore. Occurrences of

a certain sort, though they may amount to little, can be dragged
into the light—provided they throw your person into proper
relief. I will explain. If you fall out of a carriage, with no other
hurt but the scare, it's a good idea to scatter the news to the four
winds—not for the thing itself, which is insignificant, but for
the purpose of recalling a name dear to the affections of all.
You understand?"

"Yes, I understand."

"This is constant, low-price, easy, everyday publicity; but
there is another type. Whatever may be the general opinion of
the arts, it is beyond all doubt that family feeling, personal
friendship, and public esteem demand the reproduction of the
features of a loved or distinguished citizen. Nothing can keep
them from being the object of such an honor, especially if the
discernment of your friends finds no reluctance on your part. In
a case of this sort not only do the laws of common courtesy re-
quire you to accept the portrait or bust, but it would be most
inappropriate to prevent your friends from displaying it in some
public place or other.

"In this way your name becomes identified with your person.
Those who have read your speech (let's say) at the inaugural
session of the United Confederation of Hairdressers, will recognize in the steadiness of your features the author of that profound
oration, in which the 'pickaxe of progress' and the 'sweat of toil'
conquered the 'gaping jaws of poverty.'

"In the event that a committee brings the portrait to your
house, you should thank them for the civility with a speech full
of gratitude and a glass of water: it's an old, sensible, and honor-
able custom. You will then invite your best friends, your relatives, and, if possible, one or two people of social standing, to
dinner. Further, since this is a day of glory and jubilation, I
don't see how you can decently refuse a place at table to the
newspaper reporters. If the worst comes to the worst and the
duties of those gentlemen detain them elsewhere, you can help
them out to a certain extent by writing the story yourself and
sending it to the papers. And, if you have some scruple or other
—quite pardonable under the circumstances—about affixing to
your name with your own hand the descriptive adjectives it
deserves, turn the job over to one of your friends or relatives."

"I must confess, sir, what you prescribe is not at all easy."

"That's just what I've been telling you. It is difficult, it consumes time, much time, it takes years, patience, toil . . . and happy are they who reach the promised land and enter its paradise! Those who do not reach it are swallowed up in obscurity. But those who prevail! And you will prevail, believe me! You will see the walls of Jericho fall at the sound of the holy trumpets. Only then will you be able to say that you have arrived for sure. On that day you will begin your phase as an indispensable ornament, as the ticketed and labeled obligatory presence. The necessity for smelling out occasions, committees, societies, will be at an end: *they* will come to you with their great hulking air of unadjectivized substantives, and you will be the adjective of these benighted orations. You will be the *sweet odorousness* of the flowers, the *empyrean blue* of the sky, the *valued services* of the citizens, the *informative fullness* of official reports. And to be this is the main thing, because the adjective is the soul of the language, its idealistic and theoretical element. The substantive is reality naked and raw: it is the Naturalism of our vocabulary."

"And this whole career, in your opinion, is nothing more than a kind of reserve against the deficits of life?"

"That's right. It is extra. No other activity is debarred you."

"Not even politics?"

"Not even politics. It is only a question of abiding by certain essential rules and performing certain simple duties. You can belong to any party you please, liberal or conservative, republican or ultramontane, the only condition being that you do not link any special idea to those terms, and that you recognize in the one you choose merely the usefulness of the Biblical shibboleth."

"If I enter parliament can I mount the speaker's platform?"

"You can, and you should. It is a way of attracting public attention. As to the subject of your speeches, you have a choice: either petty practical matters or questions of political theory; but by all means choose the theory. Petty practical matters, one must admit, are not unsuited to that genteel dullness which is the mark of the complete stuffed shirt. But, if it is at all possible, choose theory; it is easier to handle and has more appeal. Suppose you wish to inquire into the motive for transferring the Seventh Company of Infantry from Uruguayana to Cangussú:

you will be heard only by the Minister of War, who will explain to you in ten minutes the reasons for that action. Not so with theory. A speech on political theory, by its very nature, inflames party members and the public, calls forth remarks from the galleries and answers from the rostrum. Besides, it does not obligate one to think and uncover the truth. In this branch of human knowledge all is finished, formulated, labeled, boxed: it's only a matter of reaching into the knapsack of memory. But, whatever you do, never go beyond the bounds of an enviable vulgarity."

"I'll do my best, sir. No imagination?"

"None. Rather, let the word get around that a talent in that line is decidedly low class."

"No philosophy?"

"Look, let's not beat about the bush: on paper, and on the lips, some; in reality, none. 'Philosophy of history,' for example, is an expression that you should employ with frequent regularity, but I warn you not to arrive at conclusions that have not already been reached by others. Shun everything that smells of reflection, imagination, and all that."

"Laughter too?"

"Laughter?"

"Be serious? Very serious? . . ."

"It depends. You have an idle, fun-loving nature. There's no need for you to curb it, or eliminate it; you may joke and laugh, once in a while. 'Stuffed shirt' doesn't necessarily mean 'gloomy.' A serious man may have his expansive moments. Only—and this is a ticklish point . . ."

"Yes? Go on . . ."

"Only, you must never make use of irony, that vague movement at the corner of the mouth, that thing of mystery, invented by some decadent Greek, caught by Lucian, passed on to Swift and Voltaire, a trait befitting skeptics and men of enlightenment. No . . . rather the vulgar story! Use our good old vulgar story —our friendly, smutty, fat-witted, frankly vulgar story—that has no veils or false modesty, that hits you full in the face loud as a slap with the open hand, that makes the blood leap in a man's veins and breaks his suspenders with laughing. Yes, use the vulgar story. What's that?"

"Midnight."

"Midnight? You are entering your twenty-second year, my fine gentleman. You are of age. Let's go to bed, it's late. Think over what I have told you, my boy. All things considered, this conversation of tonight is worth every bit as much as Machiavelli's *Prince*. Let's go to bed."

Translated by HELEN CALDWELL

The Holiday

The Negro servant told the schoolmaster that someone wished to see him.

"Who is it?"

"He says you don't know him, sir."

"Have him come in."

There was a general turning of heads toward the hall door, through which the unknown would enter. Soon there appeared the rude figure of a man, skin tanned by the sun, hair uncombed and too long, clothes badly wrinkled. I do not remember very clearly their color or material, but probably they were of brown denim. Everyone was waiting to hear what the man had come to say, I more than the others because it was my uncle from the country. He lived in Guaratiba. His name was Uncle Zeca.

Uncle Zeca approached the teacher and spoke to him softly. The teacher had him sit down, looked at me, and, I think, asked him something, for Uncle Zeca talked a long while, apparently making a detailed explanation. The teacher asked something else; Uncle Zeca replied; and so on, until the teacher, turning to me, said, "Mr. José Martins, you may leave."

My delight was so great that it overcame my amazement. I was ten years old, liked to play, did not like to study. A message from home, my uncle himself, my father's brother who had arrived the day before from Guaratiba—it was doubtless a party, a picnic, or something. I ran to get my hat, put my reading book in my pocket, and went down the stairs of the school, which was a little two-story building in the Rua do Senado. In the hallway I kissed Uncle Zeca's hand. In the street I tripped along, hastening my steps to keep next to him and looking up at him. He remained silent, and I lacked the courage to question him.

In a little while we arrived at my sister Felicia's school. He told me to wait, he went in, he went up, they came down, and the three of us started for home. My joy had now increased. There must certainly be a party at home, for Felicia and I were both going. We walked ahead, exchanging questions and conjectures. Maybe it was Uncle Zeca's birthday. I looked back at him; he was walking with his eyes lowered, doubtless to avoid stumbling.

On we walked. Felicia, one year older than I, wore slipper-like shoes, tied around the instep by two crossed ribbons, which ended in a bow above the ankle; my little boots of goat leather were nearly worn out. Her pantalettes were fastened at the lower ends by the shoe ribbons; my ample trousers of plain cotton wrinkled over my insteps. Now and then we would stop, she to stare at the dolls in the doorways of the little shops, I to look at some parrot, in a bistro, climbing up and down the iron chain attached to its foot. Generally, it was one I had seen before. Uncle Zeca would call us away from the observation of these manufactured and natural delights. "Come," he would say in a low voice. And we would go on, until our curiosity, aroused by some new objects, made us stop again. All the while, however, the thing uppermost in our minds was the party that was awaiting us at home.

"I don't think it's Uncle Zeca's birthday," Felicia said to me.

"Why not?"

"He looks sort of sad."

"Sad? No, not sad. He just looks serious."

"All right, serious. When a person has a birthday he looks happy."

"Then maybe it's my godfather's birthday . . ."

"Or my godmother's . . ."

"But then why did mama send us to school?"

"Maybe she didn't remember."

"There'll be a big dinner . . ."

"With dessert . . ."

"Maybe we'll dance."

We reached an agreement: it could be a party without anybody having a birthday. For example, father might have won the grand prize in the lottery. It occurred to me also that it might have something to do with the elections. My godfather was a candidate for alderman. Although I was not quite sure what a candidate or an alderman was, I had heard so much talk about the victory he was about to win that I thought it not only assured but perhaps already won. I did not know that the elections were to be held on Sunday, and now it was only Friday. I imagined bands and music, *vivas* and clapping of hands, and us children jumping, laughing, eating coconut candy. Perhaps there would be a show in the evening; I became half dizzy with anticipation. I had gone once to the theater and had returned home sound asleep, but the next day I had been so pleased with my experience that I could hardly wait to go back, although I had understood nothing that I had *heard*. I had, however, *seen* many things—elegant chairs, thrones, long lances, scenes that changed while you were looking at them, from a parlor to a forest and from the forest to a street. And the people on the stage were all princes. That is what we called people who wore silk breeches, boots or buckled shoes, swords, velvet capes, caps with feathers. Also, there was a ballet. The dancers talked with their feet and hands, exchanging positions and wearing smiles all the time. Afterwards the shouts of the audience and the clapping of hands . . .

Felicia, to whom I mentioned the possibility of a show, did not seem very excited about it, but at the same time she was not going to turn anything down. She would go to the theater. And who knows if it might not be at home, a puppet show? We were going on with these conjectures, when Uncle Zeca told us to wait; he had stopped to talk with a man.

We stopped and waited. The idea of the party, whatever its occasion, continued to excite us, me more than her. Thirty thousand things came to my mind, so precipitately that I finished the thought of none of them and so confusedly that I could not even distinguish them; quite possibly they duplicated one another. Felicia called my attention to two little colored boys wearing red stocking caps, who were going by, carrying sugar cane—which reminded us of St. Anthony's Day and St. John's Day, already passed. Then I talked to her about the bonfires in our garden, the firecrackers we had set off, the firewheels, the roman candles, and the dances with other children. If the same things would only happen this time . . . Ah! it occurred to me

that I might be able surreptitiously to drop my school book into
the fire, and hers, too, with the sewing lessons that she was learning.

"No," said Felicia.

"I want to burn my book."

"Papa would buy another."

"Until he bought it, I would have no homework to do."

We were thus engaged when we saw Uncle Zeca and the
stranger come close to us. The stranger took each of us by the
chin, lifted Felicia's face and mine, gazed at us earnestly, let us
go again, and said good-by to Uncle Zeca.

"Nine o'clock? I'll be there," he said.

"Come," said Uncle Zeca to us.

I wanted to ask him who the man was. It seemed to me that
I vaguely recognized him. Felicia thought she did, too. But his
promise to be there at nine o'clock was what interested us most.
There would surely be a party, a dance, because at nine o'clock
on ordinary nights we all went to bed. On exceptional occasions,
of course, we would stay up.

We had come to a mud puddle. I took Felicia's hand and
jumped across, so energetically that I almost dropped my book.
I looked at Uncle Zeca to see the effect. I saw him shake his
head disapprovingly. I laughed, she smiled, and we went on.

It was our day for meeting strangers. This time they were
riding on burros, and one of the two strangers was a woman.
They had come from the country. Uncle Zeca went to talk with
them in the middle of the street, after telling us to wait. The
animals stopped, of their own volition, I maintained, because
they too recognized Uncle Zeca—an idea that Felicia contra-
dicted with a gesture and that I laughingly defended. I was
really only half convinced; it was all in fun. In any event, we
both waited, examining the couple from the country. They were
thin, the woman more so than her husband, and she was also
younger; his hand was grayish. We could not hear what he and
Uncle Zeca were saying; we only saw the husband look at us with
curiosity and speak to his wife, who also looked at us, not so
much with curiosity as with pity or something very like it.
Finally, they went away, Uncle Zeca came back to us, and we
started off again for home.

Our house was on the next cross street, near the corner. On

turning the corner, we saw the entrance to the house decorated with black crepe—which filled us with amazement and fear. Instinctively, we stopped and turned our heads toward Uncle Zeca. He came to us, took each of us by the hand, and was going to say something, but it stuck in his throat; instead, he walked toward the house, still holding us by the hand. The doors of the house were half shut. I do not know whether I mentioned that we had a little store there in the front part of the house. In the street, people were standing around, curious. Through the front and side windows we could see a crowd of heads. When we arrived, there was a certain activity. Naturally my mouth was agape, as was Felicia's. Uncle Zeca pushed open one of the doors, we entered, he shut it again and went into the hallway, and we went through the dining room into the main bedroom.

Inside, near the bed, was my mother with her head buried in her hands. When she learned of our arrival, she rose with a start, came to us, and in tears embraced us, shouting, "My children, your father is dead!"

The shock was great, however much my confusion and bewilderment may have dulled the effect of the news. I had no strength to move and would have been afraid to do so. Dead—how? why? If I insert these two questions here, it is to give sequence to the narrative; at that moment I asked no questions of myself or of anyone else. I heard my mother's words, which kept repeating themselves in my mind, and her great sobs. She took hold of us and dragged us to the bed, where her husband's corpse was lying; and she made us kiss its hand. My thoughts had been so very far from all this that, in spite of all, I had at first not wholly understood; the sadness and silence of the people who surrounded the bed helped to make it clear that my father had really died. It turned out not to be a holy day with its relaxation and fun, it was not a party, it was not a case of spending glorious hours at home far from the punishments of school. I neither affirm nor deny that this fall from so pretty a dream added to my filial grief; it is best to remain silent on this point. There was father, dead, with no people jumping around, no dances, no laughter, no bands playing, all these things dead, too. If I had been told, when I left the school, why they had sent for me, obviously I would not have let the joy enter my heart, from which it was now so rudely expelled.

The funeral was the next day at nine in the morning, and probably that friend of Uncle Zeca's was there, the one who had said good-by to him on the street with a promise to be there at nine o'clock. I did not see the rites; I remember that there were people dressed in black. My godfather, owner of an import-and-export warehouse, was there, and so was his wife, who took me to a back bedroom to show me pictures. When the coffin was being taken out, I heard my mother's cries, the sound of moving feet, and some stifled words, doubtless by the persons who had hold of the handles of the coffin—"turn it sideways . . . more to the left . . . careful now . . ." Afterwards, far off, the funeral coach rolling along and the chaises behind it . . .

There went my father and my holiday! A day away from school without any fun! No, it was not *a* day but *eight,* eight days of mourning, during which the thought of returning to school sometimes occurred to me. Between condolence visits, my mother cried and sewed the mourning clothes. I cried, too; I did not see my father at the usual hours, I did not hear his words at the dinner table and store counter or the loving things he used to say to the birds. For he was a great friend of birds and kept three or four in cages. My mother said little. She spoke almost only to people from outside. In this way I learned that my father had died of apoplexy. I heard this news many times; the visitors asked about the cause of his death, and she told them everything—the time, the place, exactly what he had been doing: he had gone to get a drink of water and was filling a glass near the yard window. I learned it all by heart as a result of hearing it told so often.

Nevertheless, the boys from school managed to work their way into my imagination. One of them even asked me when I would go back.

"Saturday, my son," said my mother when I repeated the question to her; "the Mass will be Friday. No, perhaps it is just as well for you to wait until Monday."

"Saturday might be better," I suggested.

"All right," she agreed.

She was not smiling; if she could have smiled, she would have done so out of pleasure at my desire to return to school. But, knowing that I did not like school, how did she interpret my suggestion? She probably gave it some lofty significance—

guidance from heaven or from her husband. In truth, I was having no holiday, if by holiday one means a time for laughter. Nor if one means a time for relaxation, for my mother made me study, and I was miserable not only because of the studying itself but also because of the physical restrictions that it imposed. Compelled to sit, with the book in my hands, in a corner or at the table, I consigned book, table, and chair to the devil. I resorted to a trick that I recommend to the lazy; without taking my eyes from the page, I opened the door to my imagination and ran through. I set off skyrockets, listened to street organs, danced with little girls, sang, laughed, fought—lying to myself or just playing, whichever you prefer.

Once, when my mother found me in the living room and not reading, she scolded me, and I replied that I was thinking of my father. The explanation made her cry, and, indeed, it was not wholly untrue; I had been thinking about the last little present that he had given me, and I began to see him with the gift in his hand.

Felicia was as sad as I, but, to tell the truth, her chief reason was not the same. She liked to play, but did not really miss it, did not mind staying close to mother and sewing with her. Once I saw her drying mother's tears with her handkerchief. A little annoyed, I decided to imitate her and put my hand in my pocket to get my handkerchief. My hand entered the pocket without tenderness and, not finding the handkerchief, withdrew without concern. I am afraid the gesture lacked not only spontaneity but even sincerity.

Do not censure me. I had gone through long days of silence and seclusion. I wanted to go just once to the little store, which had opened again after the funeral and where the salesman continued to serve customers. I would talk with him, would watch the sale of needles and thread and the measurement of ribbons, would go to the entrance, to the sidewalk, to the corner of the street . . . My mother smothered this dream in its infancy. I had hardly reached the counter when she sent the slave to get me; off I went to the rear part of the house and to my studies. I pulled my hair, I clenched my fists; I do not remember whether I wept with rage.

My book reminded me of school, and the thought of school consoled me. By then I had developed real nostalgia for it. I saw from afar the boys' faces, our fooling around on the benches, and our leaps and jumps when we went out. I felt myself struck in the face by one of those paper spitballs with which we used to rouse each other, and I made one and threw it at my supposed rouser. The spitball, as sometimes used to happen, fell on the head of a third student, who quickly avenged himself. Some, more timid, confined themselves to making faces. These thoughts did not provide complete satisfaction, but they helped. The state of exile that, with Uncle Zeca, I had so joyfully left, now seemed to me to be far-off heaven, and I was afraid I might lose it. No party at home, few words, almost no activity. During these days more than ever, I drew cats in pencil in the margins of the reading book; cats and pigs. It did not make me happy, but it distracted me.

After the seventh-day Mass, I was back on the street. On Saturday I did not go to school, I went to my godfather's house, where I could talk a little more, and on Sunday I stood at the entrance to the store. It was not complete happiness. Complete happiness came on Monday, in school. I entered dressed in black and was gazed upon with curiosity, but I was so delighted to be in the midst of my fellow students that my holiday *sans* joy was soon forgotten, and I found a great joy *sans* holiday.

Translated by William L. Grossman

Admiral's Night

At three o'clock in the afternoon Deolindo the Nostril (a sobriquet given him by his crew mates) left the Navy Yard and walked briskly up the Rua de Bragança. His corvette had just returned from a long training cruise; he came ashore as soon as he could obtain leave. His friends had said to him, laughing:

"Hey, Nostril! You're going to have a real Admiral's Night, aren't you? Wine, a guitar, and Genoveva's arms. Genoveva's loving little . . ."

Deolindo had smiled. Exactly so: an Admiral's Night, as the phrase goes, was awaiting him on shore. The passion had begun three months before the corvette's departure. Genoveva was a brown-skinned girl from the country, twenty years old, with dark, knowing eyes. They had met at a friend's house and had fallen madly in love, so madly that they had been on the point of doing a mad thing: he was going to desert the Navy, and she was going to run away with him to the most remote village in the interior.

Old Ignacia, with whom Genoveva lived, had dissuaded them. Hence Deolindo had decided to follow orders and sail on the training cruise. As a mutual guaranty they had decided that they ought to take an oath of fidelity.

"I swear by God in heaven. And you?"

"I also."

"Say it."

"I swear by God in heaven. May the holy light fail me at the hour of death."

The meeting of minds was duly celebrated. No one could doubt their sincerity; she cried like one possessed, he bit his lip to conceal his emotion. Finally they parted. Genoveva watched the corvette sail off and returned home with such tension in her heart that it seemed as though something dreadful was going to happen, but nothing did. The days went by, the weeks, the months, ten months, then the corvette returned and Deolindo with it.

There he goes now, up the Rua de Bragança, through Prainha and Saude, until he comes to Gambôa, where Genoveva lives, just beyond the English cemetery. There he will probably find her leaning on the window sill, waiting for him. Deolindo prepares a few words with which to greet her. He has already composed this: "I took an oath and I kept it," but he is working on something better. He remembers women he saw all over the world: Italian, Marseillaise, Turkish, many of them pretty or at least so they seemed to him. Not all, he concedes, were exactly his dish, but some of them certainly were, and even so they did not really interest him. He thought only of Genoveva. Her house, her sweet little house, its walls cracked by the sun, and its sparse, old, broken-down furniture, these he remembered when he stood before exotic palaces in distant lands. By considerable abnegation he bought in Trieste a pair of earrings, which he now carries in his pocket together with some less impressive little gifts. And what is she going to give him? Very likely a handkerchief embroidered with his name and with an anchor in the corner, for she is very clever at embroidery.

About this time he arrived in Gambôa, passed the cemetery, and stopped at the house. The door was closed. He knocked and immediately heard a familiar voice, that of old Ignacia, who opened the door with exclamations of great surprise. Deolindo, impatient, asked for Genoveva.

"Don't talk about that crazy girl," said the old woman. "I'm glad about the advice I gave you. See, she's gone off."

"But what was it? What happened?"

The old woman told him to take it easy, it was nothing, just one of those things that happen. It was not worth getting angry about. Genoveva's head was turned . . .

"Who turned it?"

"Did you know José Diogo, the cloth peddler? She's with him. You can't imagine how in love they are. She's like a crazy girl. That's why we had a fight. José Diogo would never go home. They'd whisper and whisper, until one day I said I didn't want my house to get a bad name. Good Father in heaven, it was a day of judgment! Genoveva glared at me with eyes this size, saying that she never gave anyone a bad name and that she didn't need charity. What do you mean, charity, Genoveva? All I said was I don't want whispering at my door until six o'clock at night. . . . Two days later she moved away and never spoke to me again."

"Where is she living?"

"On Formosa Beach, before you come to the quarry. The house has just been painted."

Deolindo had heard enough. Old Ignacia, a little sorry she had spoken so freely, advised prudence, but he did not listen. Off he went. I shall not relate his thoughts on the way, for they were wholly disorganized. Ideas navigated about his brain as in a tempest, amid a confusion of winds and foghorns. Among them gleamed a sailor's knife, vengeful and bloody. He had passed through Gambôa and the Sacco de Alferes, and had entered Formosa Beach. He did not know the number of the house, but knew that it was near the quarry and freshly painted, and with the help of people in the neighborhood he would find it. He had no reason to foresee that chance would take hold of Genoveva and seat her at the window, sewing, at the very moment when he came along. He saw her and stopped. She, seeing the form of a man, raised her eyes and recognized the sailor.

"Of all things!" she exclaimed in surprise. "When did you get back? Come in, Deolindo."

And, rising, she opened the door and let him in. Any man would have become wild with hope, so frank and friendly was the girl's manner. Maybe the old woman had been mistaken or had lied. Maybe, even, the peddler's song had ended. All this indeed passed through Deolindo's mind, without the exact form of reason but swiftly and tumultuously. Genoveva left the door open, had him sit down, asked about the voyage, and said that she thought he had gained weight; no emotion, no intimacy. Deolindo lost all hope. He had no knife with him, but he had his hands; Genoveva was a small piece of woman, he could easily strangle her. For the first few moments he thought of nothing else.

"I know everything," he said.

"Who told you?"

Deolindo shrugged his shoulders.

"Whoever it was," she continued, "did they tell you I was in love with somebody?"

"Yes."

"They told you the truth."

Deolindo started toward her, but the way she looked at him made him stop. Then she said that if she let him in, it was because she thought him an intelligent man. She told him everything, how terribly she had missed him, the propositions the peddler had made, her refusals, until one morning, without knowing how or why, she had awakened in love with him.

"Really, I thought of you a lot. Just ask Ignacia how much I cried. . . . But my heart changed. . . . It changed . . . I'm telling you all this as if I were talking to a priest," she concluded, smiling.

She was not smiling in mockery. Her manner of speech suggested a combination of candor and cynicism, insolence and simplicity; I cannot explain it better. Perhaps the words insolence and cynicism are poorly chosen. Genoveva was not defending herself at all, she had no moral standards to indicate a need for defense. What she was saying, in brief, was that it would have been better not to have changed, that she had really loved him or she would not have been willing to run away with him; but that, as José Diogo had intervened and conquered, one might as well accept the fact. The poor sailor cited the parting oath as an eternal obligation, because of which he had agreed not to desert his ship: "I swear by God in heaven. May the holy light fail me at the hour of death." He had been willing to sail only because she had sworn this oath. With those words in his ears he had gone, traveled, waited, and returned; they had given him the strength to live. I swear by God in heaven. May the holy light fail me at the hour of death . . .

"Yes, all right, Deolindo; it was the truth. When I swore it, it was the truth. I even wanted to run away with you. But then other things happened . . . this fellow came along and I began to like him . . ."

"But that's just why people swear not to, so that they won't like anybody else . . ."

"Stop it, Deolindo. Did you never think of anyone but me? Don't talk nonsense . . ."

"When will José Diogo come back?"

"He's not coming back today."

"No?"

"He's not coming. He's working in Guaratiba. He'll probably be back Friday or Saturday. . . . Why do you want to know? What did he ever do to you?"

Perhaps any other woman would have said substantially the same thing, but few would have expressed it so candidly. See how close to nature we are at this point. What did he ever do to you? What did this rock that fell on your head ever do to you? Any physicist can explain why a rock falls; it has nothing to do with you.

Deolindo declared, with a desperate gesture, that he wanted to kill the peddler. Genoveva looked at him with contempt, smiled slightly, and made a deprecative cluck with her tongue. And when he accused her of ingratitude and lying, she could not conceal her amazement. What lying? What ingratitude? Had she not already told him that what she swore was the truth? The Virgin there on top of the bureau, she knew it was the truth. Is this how he repaid her for her suffering? And he who talked so much about fidelity, had he always thought of her wherever he went?

His answer was to put his hand in his pocket and take out the package he had brought. She opened it, looked at the gifts one by one, and finally came upon the earrings. They were not, they could not be, expensive; they were even in poor taste; but they were glorious to behold. Genoveva took them in her fingers, happy, dazzled, examined one side and then the other, closely and at arm's length, and finally put them on. Then, to appraise their effect, she looked in the ten-cent mirror hanging on the wall between the window and the door. She stepped back, approached the mirror again, turned her head from side to side.

"They're very pretty, very!" she said, bowing her thanks. "Where did you buy them?"

He did not reply. Indeed, he had no time to do so, for she fired two or three more questions at him, one right after the other, so confused was she at receiving a wonderful gift in exchange for having fallen out of love with him. Confusion for five or four minutes; maybe two. Then she took off the earrings, contemplated them, and put them in the little box on the round table in the middle of the room. He, for his part, began to think that, just as he had lost her because of his absence, so now the other might lose her; and probably she had sworn no oath at all to the peddler.

"Talking and fooling around all afternoon, and now it's night already," said Genoveva.

Indeed, night was swiftly falling. One could no longer see the Lepers' Hospital and could hardly make out Melon Island; even the rowboats and canoes in front of the house blended with the mud of the beach. Genoveva lit a candle. Then she sat down and asked him to tell her something about the countries he had seen. Deolindo refused. He said he was going; he rose and took a few steps. But the demon of hope was biting the poor devil's heart; he sat down and began to talk about his experiences on the voyage. Genoveva listened attentively. Interrupted by the entrance of a woman friend who lived near by, Genoveva asked her to sit down, too, and listen to "the pretty stories Deolindo is telling"; there was no other introduction. The grand lady who lies awake into the morning because she cannot put down the novel she is reading does not live the lives of the characters in it more intimately than the sailor's ex-lover was living the scenes that he narrated; she was as freely absorbed as if there had been nothing between them but the telling of a story. What matters to the grand lady the author of the book? What mattered to this girl the teller of the tales?

Hope, meanwhile, had begun to desert him, and he rose, once and for all, to leave. Genoveva did not want to let him go until her friend had seen the earrings; she showed them to her with comments on their beauty and value. The other woman was enchanted, praised them highly, asked whether he had bought them in France, and requested Genoveva to put them on.

"Really, they're beautiful."

I guess the sailor shared this opinion. He liked to look at them, found them to be virtually made for her, and for a few seconds tasted the rare and delicate pleasure of having made a fine gift; but for only a few seconds.

As he was saying good-by, Genoveva accompanied him to the door to thank him once more for the gift and probably to say some politely kind words. Her friend, whom she had left in the room, heard only, "Don't be foolish, Deolindo"; and from the sailor, "You'll see." She could not hear the rest, which was spoken in whispers.

Deolindo walked off along the beach, downcast and slow, no longer the impetuous youth of the afternoon but sorrowful and old or, to use a metaphor common among our sailors, halfway down the deep shore. Genoveva went back indoors, bustling and chatty. She told the woman about her naval romance, praised greatly Deolindo's character and fine manners. Her friend declared that she found him very charming.

"A really nice boy," repeated Genoveva. "Do you know what he just told me?"

"What?"

"That he's going to kill himself."

"Jesus!"

"Don't worry, he won't really. That's how Deolindo is: he says things but he doesn't do them. You'll see, he won't kill himself. Poor thing, he's jealous. . . . The earrings are gorgeous."

"I never saw any like them here in Rio."

"Neither did I," said Genoveva, examining them in the light. Then she put them away and invited the woman to sew with her. "Let's sew awhile, I want to finish my blue camisole . . ."

She was right: the sailor did not kill himself. The next day some of his mates slapped him on the shoulder, congratulating him on his Admiral's Night, and asked about Genoveva, whether she had cried a lot during his absence, whether she was still pretty. . . . He replied to everything with a sly and satisfied smile, the smile of a man tasting inwardly the memories of the night before.

Translated by William L. Grossman

Final Request

". . . Item, it is my last wish that the coffin in which my body is buried be made in the shop of Joaquim Soares on the Rua da Alfândega. I wish him to be informed of this disposition, which shall also be made public. Joaquim Soares does not know me; but he is worthy of the honor, as one of our finest craftsmen and one of the most highly respected men in the land . . ."

This provision of the will was carried out to the letter. Joaquim Soares made the coffin in which poor Nicolau B. de C.'s body was placed. He made it *con amore,* and, finally, in an access of cordiality he begged to be allowed to do it without pay. He was already paid, he said: the mark of favor shown him by the deceased was in itself a notable prize. All he wanted was an exact copy of the paragraph in the will. They gave it to him. He had it framed, and hung it up on a nail in his shop. The other coffinmakers, once their astonishment had passed, protested that the will was a piece of nonsense. Happily—and this is one of the advantages of an organized society—happily, all the other trades and professions thought that this hand, reaching forth from the pit to bless the work of a modest craftsman, performed an act of rare magnanimity. It was in 1855: people were closer then, nobody talked of anything else. The name of Nicolau reverberated for many days in the press of the imperial capital; from there it passed to the provinces. But the life of all of us is full of change, events crowd one upon the other so fast, and, finally, the memory of men is so flimsy, that a day arrived when Nicolau's act was completely sunk in oblivion.

I am not here to restore it. To forget is a necessity. Life is a slate, which destiny, in order to write down a new event, must wipe clean of the one written there. A matter of pencil and sponge. No, no, I am not here to restore it. There are thousands of actions just as handsome, or even more handsome than Nicolau's, that have been eaten away by forgetfulness. I have come to tell you that the provision in the will was not an effect without a cause. I have come to describe one of the most morbid curiosities of this century.

Yes, dear reader, we are going to enter full blast into pathology. That little boy you see there toward the end of the last century (when Nicolau died in 1855 he was sixty-eight years old), that little boy was not a sound fruit, he was not a perfect organism. On the contrary, from his tenderest years, he showed by acts repeated time and again that there was deep within him a hidden deformity, an organic flaw. One cannot explain in any other way the persistence with which he would run to destroy the playthings of other little boys. I do not mean toys as good as his or worse than his, but ones that were better or more expensive than his. Still less can one understand why, when the toy was unique, or perhaps only rare, he consoled the victim with two or three kicks, never less than one. All this is obscure. It could not have been his father's fault. His father was an honest shopkeeper or commission man (most of the persons in this city that are given the title of *merchants,* the Marquis de Lavradio used to say, are nothing more than simple commission men) who lived with a certain pomp in the last quarter of the century, a gruff, austere man, who admonished his son, and, when necessary, punished him. But neither admonishings nor punishments had any effect. Nicolau's inner urge produced more effect than any paternal cane, and once or twice a week the little boy slipped back into his criminal ways. The family was deeply disturbed. There was one instance which, in view of its grave consequences, deserves to be told.

The viceroy, at that time the Count de Rezende, was plagued by the necessity of constructing a dock at Dom Manuel beach. This, which today would be a simple municipal episode, was, in those days in a city of sparse population, an important undertaking. The viceroy had no funds; the public coffers could scarcely meet the ordinary demands upon them. A statesman, and probably a philosopher, the count devised an expedient no less pleasant than profitable: namely, the distribution, in ex-

change for pecuniary donations, of the posts of captain, lieutenant, and second lieutenant.

When the decree was made public, Nicolau's father saw at
once that this was an opportunity to figure, without personal
danger, in the military gallery of the age and at the same time to
disprove one of the teachings of the Brahmins. For it is written
in the laws of Manu that from the arms of Brahma were born
the warriors, and from his belly the farmers and merchants.
When Nicolau's father received his captain's commission he corrected this point of class anatomy.

Another merchant, who competed with him in everything,
though they were close friends, heard of the appointment and
went to take his stone to the dock also. Unluckily, pique at being
a few days behind, prompted him to make a request that was not
only in bad taste but, as it turned out, most unfortunate. *He*
asked the viceroy to grant a second dock officer's commission
(this was the title given to those decorated by this system) to his
seven-year-old son. The viceroy hesitated; but the applicant, in
addition to the double donation, had influence, and the child
came away with the rank of second lieutenant.

It was all done in the greatest secrecy. Nicolau's father did
not get wind of the matter till the next Sunday at the Carmo
church, where he saw the two of them, father and son, and the
boy decked out in a small-size but dashing uniform. Nicolau,
who was also there, became livid. In a flash, he threw himself on
the young lieutenant and tore his uniform before the parents
could come to the rescue. A scandal. The clamor of the mob, the
indignation of the devout, and the groans of the victim interrupted the divine service for several minutes. The fathers exchanged several sharp words outside the church door, and remained enemies for life.

"That boy of ours will be the death of us!" shouted Nicolau's
father when they got home.

Nicolau got a thrashing, suffered great pain, wept, sobbed;
but in the way of improvement? Nothing. Other little boys' playthings were in no less danger. It was the same with their clothes.
The more wealthy children of the neighborhood never went outside except in the most inexpensive play clothes, the only way
of escaping Nicolau's nails. With the passing of time he extended
his aversion to the faces themselves when they were handsome,

or considered as such. The street on which he lived boasted an untold number of bruised, scratched, spat-upon faces. Things reached such a pass that his father decided to keep him shut up in the house for three or four months. It was a palliative, and as such excellent. As long as the incarceration lasted, Nicolau was nothing less than angelic. Aside from that morbid habit of his, he was gentle, docile, obedient, fond of his family, regular in his prayers. At the end of four months his father let him loose. It was time to put him in grammar school.

"Leave him with me," said the teacher, "and with that." He pointed to the ferule . . . "With that it is unlikely he will have an urge to mistreat his companions."

Frivolous, thrice-frivolous teacher! Yes, there is no doubt he succeeded in protecting the handsome little boys and the fancy clothes by punishing poor Nicolau's first onslaughts, but in what respect did this cure him of the malady? On the contrary, obliged to hold himself in, to swallow his impulse, he suffered double, he would become more livid than before—with an overtone of verdigris. Sometimes he was forced to turn away his eyes, or close them, so as not to burst, he said. And, if he left off persecuting the best-looking or best-dressed, he did not spare those who were ahead in their studies: he pommeled them, snatched their books and threw them away on the beach or into the swamp. Brawls, bloodshed, hatreds—these were life's fruits for him, and besides he suffered cruel pain—pain that his family refused to understand. If we add that he could not study anything continuously but only piecemeal and poorly, as tramps eat, nothing regular, nothing methodical, we will have seen some of the distressing consequences of this hidden, morbid condition. His father had cherished the idea of sending his son to the university. When he found himself forced to strangle this dream also, he was ready to curse Nicolau; it was his mother who saved him.

One century departed, another came into being, but the lesion in Nicolau's organism remained. His father died in 1807, his mother in 1809. Three months later his sister married a Dutch physician. Nicolau now lived by himself. He was twenty-three years old, a dandy and man about town—but of a peculiar sort. He could not meet another of his set who either had more noble features or was wearing a specially fine waistcoat, without experiencing a violent pain, so violent that he sometimes had to bite his lip till it bled. Other times his legs grew wobbly and he reeled, or from the corner of his mouth there trickled an almost imperceptible thread of foam. The rest was no less cruel. He would be disgruntled; at home everything seemed bad, uncomfortable, loathsome. He hit the slaves on the head with plates, which were also broken, and kicked the dogs; he was not quiet ten minutes; he did not eat, or only a little. Finally he would go to bed. Sleep repaired everything. He woke up affable and kind, soul of a patriarch blessing all, kissing the dogs between the ears, letting them lick his face, giving them the best he had, calling the slaves the most intimate and endearing things. And all, dogs and slaves, forgot the blows of the night before, and ran at his call, obedient, adoring, as if this were the true master, and not that other man.

One day when he was at his sister's she asked him why he did not take up some career or other, something to occupy his . . .

"You are right," he said, "I'll look into it."

His brother-in-law chimed in and suggested the diplomatic service. The brother-in-law had begun to suspect he was suffering from some illness and thought a change of climate would restore him to health. Nicolau secured a letter of introduction and went to see the Minister of Foreign Affairs. He found him surrounded by several subsecretaries, on the point of leaving for the palace to bring the news of the second fall of Napoleon, news that had arrived a few minutes before. The presence of the minister, the solemnity of the moment, the bowing and scraping of the secretaries, all this so struck at Nicolau's heart that he could not look the minister in the face. He tried, six or eight times, to lift his eyes, and the one time he succeeded they were so crossed that he saw no one, or only a shadow, a shape, that hurt his pupils; at the same time, his face turned green. He stepped back, extended a trembling hand to the draperies in the doorway, and fled.

"I don't want to be anything," he said to his sister when he got home. "I have you and my friends."

The "friends" were the most obnoxious young men in the city, commonplace and coarse. Nicolau had chosen them carefully. To live without the company of the important men of the community was a great sacrifice for him, but, since he would have suffered much more living with them, he put up with it. This proves that he had a certain empirical understanding of his malady and of the way to relieve it. With those companions of his, all Nicolau's physiological disorders vanished. He could gaze at them without becoming livid, without squinting, without his legs giving way, without anything. Besides, they not only spared his natural irritability, they exerted themselves to render his life, if not pleasant, at least calm. And to this end they kept paying him the finest compliments/in the world, in fawning attitudes, or with a certain obsequious familiarity. Nicolau loved inferior natures in general, as the sick love the drug that restores them to health: he petted them in a fatherly manner, heaped them with affectionate praise, lent them money, presented them with delicate and thoughtful gifts, opened up his heart to them . . .

Then came the Shout of Independence at Ypiringa. Nicolau entered politics. The year 1823 found him in the Constituent Assembly. Words cannot describe the way he fulfilled the duties of his post. An upright, disinterested patriot! But it was not without cost that he practiced these public virtues; it was only at the price of great spiritual turbulence. Speaking metaphorically, one may say that the meetings of the assembly cost him precious blood. It was not only because the debates seemed intolerable, but also because it was hard for him to look at certain men, especially on certain days. Montezuma, for example, seemed flabby to him, Vergueiro crude, the Andradas detestable. Each speech, not only of the leading orators, but even of the second-rate ones, was a genuine torture for him. Still, he remained steadfast, punctual. The balloting never found him absent, his name never sounded through the august chamber without an echo. Whatever might be his own desperation, he was able to contain himself and place the idea of country above his own comfort. It may be that in his heart he applauded the decree for dissolution. I do not affirm it, but there is good reason to believe that Nicolau, in spite of outward appearances, enjoyed seeing the assembly dispersed. And, if that conjecture is true, this one will be no less so—that the deportation of some of the Constituent leaders, who were declared enemies of the people, damped that pleasure. Nicolau, who had suffered from their speeches, suffered no less from their exile, inasmuch as it gave them a certain importance. If only he, too, had been exiled!

"You could get married, brother," his sister said to him.

"I don't have a bride."

"I'll get you one. Shall I?"

It was a scheme of her husband's. In his opinion the nature of Nicolau's malady was plain: it was a worm in his spleen that fed on the pain of the patient, that is to say, on a special secretion produced by the sight of certain acts, situations, or persons. It was only a question of killing the worm; but, since he did not know of any chemical substance capable of destroying it, his only recourse was to prevent the secretion—which would produce the same effect. He therefore urged Nicolau to marry some pretty and accomplished girl, to leave the city, and get a place in the country, to which he would take his finest table ware, finest furniture, most disreputable friends, et cetera.

"Every morning," the brother-in-law confided to his wife, "Nicolau will receive a newspaper that I shall have specially printed for the sole purpose of telling him the most agreeable things in the world, and naming them one by one, recalling his modest but helpful labors in the Constituent Assembly, and imputing to him many amorous adventures, flashes of keen-wittedness, and acts of courage. I have already spoken to the Dutch admiral about having some of our officers wait on Nicolau, from time to time, to tell him they cannot return to The Hague without having the honor of meeting such an eminent and charming citizen, in whom are united rare qualities ordinarily scattered over many individuals. Now you, if you can get some modiste, Gudin for example, to name a hat or a little ruffled cape after Nicolau, it would be of great help in the cure of your dear brother. Anonymous love letters sent through the mail are an effective remedy . . . But let us begin with the beginning, that is, to marry him."

Never was a plan more conscientiously carried out. The bride chosen for him was the most elegant, or one of the most elegant, in the capital. The bishop himself married them. When they withdrew to the country, only some of Nicolau's most worthless friends went along. The newspaper was fabricated, the love letters sent, the official visits duly paid. For three months everything worked like a charm. But nature, sworn to cheat and cozen man, once more showed that she possesses surprising hidden powers.

One of the ways of giving pleasure to Nicolau was to praise the beauty, elegance, and virtues of his wife; but the disease had progressed, and what should have been an excellent medicine was a simple aggravation of the complaint. After a certain length of time Nicolau began to find all these eulogies of his wife otiose and excessive. And this was enough to exasperate him, and exasperation produced the deadly secretion. It seems he even reached a point where he could not look at her for very long, and scarcely ever did look at her. Then there occurred several rows, which would have been the beginning of a separation if she had not shortly died. Nicolau's grief was profound and genuine, but the cure was interrupted because he went back to Rio de Janeiro, where we find him some time later among the revolutionaries of 1831.

Although it may seem rash to suggest the reasons that led Nicolau to the Campo da Acclamação on the night of the sixth of April, I believe one will not be far from the truth if he supposes (it is the reasoning of a famous though anonymous Athenian) that those who spoke well and those who spoke ill of the Emperor Pedro I were equally satisfactory to Nicolau. That man, who inspired enthusiasms and hatreds, whose name was repeated wherever Nicolau went, on the street, in the theater, in other people's houses, became a real, morbid persecution. Hence the fervor with which he joined the sedition of 1831. The abdication brought him relief. The truth is, however, that the Regency soon found him among its opponents. And there are those who claim he joined the Caramurú or restoration party, even though there is no proof of it. What is certain is that Nicolau's public life ceased with the majority of Pedro II.

The disease had now definitely taken control of the organism. Little by little Nicolau went into seclusion. He could not pay certain calls, visit certain houses. The theater failed to distract him. The state of his auditory organs was so delicate that the sound of applause caused him excruciating pains. The enthusiasm of the Rio population for the famous Candiani, and also for Meréa, but mainly for Candiani, whose carriage was drawn by human arms—a civility all the more remarkable in that they would not have done it for Plato himself—this enthusiasm was one of Nicolau's greatest torments. Finally, he almost stopped going to the theater, found Candiani intolerable, and preferred the *Norma* of the hurdy-gurdies to that of the prima donna. It was not from an exaggerated patriotism that he enjoyed seeing

João Caetano in the early days. But finally he abandoned him
too, and along with him well nigh all the theater.

"He is lost!" thought his brother-in-law. "If we could only give
him a new spleen . . ."

How could he imagine such a foolish thing? Nicolau was lost,
naturally—destroyed by nature herself. Domestic pleasures no
longer contented him. His literary attempts—family verses, prize
impromptu poems, political stanzas—had not lasted long, and it
may even be that they hastened the progress of the malady. In
any case, it struck him one day that this occupation was the most
ridiculous thing in the world and the adulation of Gonçalves
Dias, for example, showed him a nation of vulgarity and bad
taste. This literary sentiment, result of an organic lesion, reacted
on this lesion in such a way as to produce serious crises that
confined him to his bed for a time. His brother-in-law seized the
moment to clear the house of all books of a certain caliber.

More difficult to explain is the sloppy way he began to dress a
few months thereafter. Brought up in habits of stylish elegance,
he was an old customer of one of the leading court tailors, Plum,
and he never let a day pass without having his hair dressed at the
establishment of Demarais & Gérard, *coiffeurs de la cour,* on the
Rua do Ouvidor. It seems he found this designation of "hairdressers to the court" conceited, and rebuked them by going to
a low-class barber to have his hair dressed. As for the motive that
led him to change his way of dress, I repeat, it is entirely obscure, and, unless it can be attributed to age, inexplicable.

The dismissal of his cook is another enigma. At the urging of
his brother-in-law, who wanted to keep him diverted, Nicolau
gave two dinners a week, and the guests were unanimous in the
opinion that his cook surpassed all the others of the capital.
Actually his dishes were good, a few excellent, but the praise was
a bit emphatic, a bit excessive, for the very purpose of giving
pleasure to Nicolau, and it did for a certain length of time. How
can you explain then the fact that one Sunday, as soon as dinner
was over, a magnificent dinner, he fired this worthy and remarkable man who had been the indirect cause of some of his most
delightful moments on earth? An impenetrable mystery.

"He was a thief!" was the reply Nicolau gave his brother-in-
law.

Neither the efforts of the latter, nor those of his sister and of

his friends, nor his wealth, or anything, improved our poor Nicolau. The secretion in the spleen became incessant, and the worm
multiplied by the millions . . . I do not know whether this theory is the true one, but after all it was his brother-in-law's. His
last years were excruciating. He turned green, was constantly
irritated, squint-eyed, suffering more himself than he made others
suffer. The least or greatest thing pulverized his nerves: a good
speech, a clever artist, a carriage, a cravat, a sonnet, a witty
remark, an interesting dream, everything, brought on an attack.

Had he determined to let himself die? One would imagine so
to see the impassivity with which he refused the remedies of the
leading physicians of the capital. Finally it was necessary to
resort to deception and give them as if they had been prescribed
by some quack. But it was too late. Death carried him off in a
couple of weeks.

"Joaquim Soares?" shouted the brother-in-law in astonishment
when he learned of the provision in the dead man's will specify-
ing that his coffin be made by this workman. "But that fellow's
coffins aren't worth a damn, and . . ."

"Hush!" interrupted his wife. "Our dear brother's wish must
be respected."

Translated by HELEN CALDWELL

These twelve stories by Brazil's greatest writer are penetrating psychological vignettes, and witty ironic satires on science, politics, the gambling instinct, the professorial mind, as well as that of the lady of easy virtue, sadism, envy, and other human foibles and vanities. Here is Machado de Assis' humor in both its mild and mordant form; all the stories, no matter how grim the message, contain powerful comic elements and are cast in the mold of comedy. The locale of all the stories is Rio de Janeiro or its outskirts.

"The first collection of Machado's short stories to appear in English, and these 12 peculiar 'comedies,' at once sophisticated and intense, caustic and tender, allow one to wonder why on earth we have had to wait so long....The translation reads remarkably smoothly."
—*The Guardian*

"These stories—so ably translated—are of a piece with the novels that have established Machado's reputation in this country. . . . All contain profound reverberations beneath their witty exterior; all probe significant elements of the human situation while effortlessly unrolling seemingly commonplace plots; all explore the depths of man's experience with both understatement and sympathy."